# The Old World

BOOKS BY
JONATHAN STRONG

—————

*Tike and Five Stories*
*Ourselves*
*Elsewhere*
*Secret Words*
*Companion Pieces*
*An Untold Tale*
*Offspring*

# The Old World

A NOVEL

JONATHAN
STRONG

### Z
ZOLAND BOOKS
*Cambridge, Massachusetts*

First edition published in 1997 by
Zoland Books, Inc.
384 Huron Avenue
Cambridge, Massachusetts 02138

Cover design by Glenn Suokko
Book design by Boskydell Studio
Printed in the United States of America

04 03 02 01 00 99 98     8 7 6 5 4 3 2

This book is printed on acid-free paper, and its binding
materials have been chosen for strength and durability.

*Library of Congress Cataloging-in-Publication Data*

Strong, Jonathan.
The old world : a novel / by Jonathan Strong.
p.     cm.
ISBN 0-944072-81-x (pbk.: alk. paper)
I. Title.
PS3569.T698O38   1997
813'.54—dc21
97-3166
CIP

*To the memory of*
MARC ROY ELLEDGE
1958–1992

PART ONE

# Invocation

**D**EAREST ONE—

We want to tell you what's become of us.

Once we helped you maintain a refuge in an unsympathetic world. In your classroom, you used to draw us to you: *Dear ones, my dear ones — how may I put it best in English? — my dearest ones.* Remember us, Anna?

We are thinking of that fervid mind of yours. Somewhere mustn't it still be hurtling on in its forward course? How could your mind ever have pulled itself up short, trembled, and sunk with your mere body? No, it must have shattered your skull apart, broken you (the essential you) free to soar ahead. Haven't you been just beyond us, just ahead out of our sight, for twenty-five years?

But now a peripeteia (your great word) is trembling under us too. *I will explain, children, so you may recognize it. A moment of reversal, as if an automobile is braking, but, oh God, too late! You are first falling ahead then sinking back, the stomach all hollow, that is how it feels.* As for your own airborne hovering moment, Anna: we still gulp at the memory of it.

You'd been our teacher. It doesn't really seem so long ago. *But all stories are about time,* you once told us, as if that should have been perfectly evident. You made us feel that everything true should be evident, for how else could it be? Even the gender of a noun: *But, dearest ones, of course it's feminine.* You drove us crazy often enough.

But: *All stories are about time,* you found yourself explaining to four high school boys in Quissick, Massachusetts, the Upholstery City, in the year 1961. *What's been young,* you said to us in eleventh grade, *must become older, even if only by an hour. Even the story that begins after it is all done, it is about time too, children, but* (delight in your eyes) *looking backwards across it.*

Anna, we took furious notes. We couldn't always tell when you meant to be funny.

Then, with us lingering at the classroom door: *So by the end of reading, dear ones, you also are never as you were. It takes time to read, and you've changed too. You've been put through, maybe, a structure of time. As in a piece of music, time marked in measures, isn't it, Henry? You can never hear it all at once. You must go through it.*

We want to tell you what we've gone through since we were all together in that old world when you were our relentless questioner.

*Do you hear that voice, children? Who is it speaking? No, by God, but don't be idiotic. I mean underneath, dear ones. Whose voice is that?*

We're still listening, Anna. Can you hear us?

Perhaps you catch only one voice, commingled, over such a distance. We're close to each other again but, here, so far from you. We want to tell you now things you couldn't have imagined. Along with us, the whole world is very much changed.

But that summer of your death, for a time, we continued in our recognizable ways. Another day, another hour — no more change than that. Stunned, but little had cracked open inside us yet: Malcolm wandered the mountain, biked the back roads — he'd be off to Boston to start college in September; Henry took on an extra shift at the lumberyard to be able to afford his own apartment — you'd said he must move out from home; Kip was already taking the summer session at Quissick State (English Romantics, American Transcendentalists) but he'd have been reading books all the time anyway, wouldn't he? We were baffled in our mourning for you, Anna, unwilling quite to feel it. Don't resent us. Only Rupert, as you might have predicted, showed the sudden loss of you in everything he did. He went thumbing out the Worcester Road, the road to Southbridge or to Orange, he'd end up wherever he was taken and see what happened to him next, as if he no longer had any choices of his own.

You never saw what Rupert came from, did you, Anna, never visited him at home because he had no parents to invite you. Besides, Rupert and his aunt themselves never ate at the broad oak table under the dusty chandelier with half its crystal baubles missing. He'd gulp something at their kitchen counter and leave a bowl of soup by his aunt's chair for her to slurp. Plashing Falls is still the lost part of town, Anna, but those empty high-ceilinged brick row houses, those boarded-up shells, those caverns behind smashed windows, they're all cut up into tiny apartments now, mostly filled with Asian refugees, and on one corner the Vongpranith Convenience and Oriental Market. *Well, I'd like to hear what certain Quissick people make of that,* you'll say. *But tell me, children — Asians? Refugees from what?* Anna, we can't begin to tell you.

Back in your day, our day with you, Rupert slouched about lonesome in slummy Plashing Falls, the only kid on his half-inhabited block. His aunt, all day in her chair, could no longer stumble her way up to the second floor, so she slept on a mahogany four-poster in the front room, heavy curtains drawn at all hours. Not even fifty yet and arthritis crippling her — depressed, a little crazy, she'd shuffle around to spy between the curtains at the boozers across the street. She'd pass a feather duster along tabletop or chair back leaving at best a darker stripe. But the floors above, Anna, were Rupert's alone, where he could hide out and his aunt could never catch him.

Rupert once did ask her if she would like to meet Anna Aylmer; after all, you were her compatriot. "Never!" she shouted back at him, because she mistook what had brought you from the Old World. Her confused notions set her ruminating, casting suspicious glances at her own shoulder (a nervous tic) and mumbling speculations her nephew never stuck around long enough to hear: "I tell you, Rupert, she was a Red whore to soldiers in Spain, so it is, this German woman who teaches Spanish. Rupert?" But he'd have motioned whichever after-school pal was with him off to his own territory upstairs, beyond her mumbles and glances.

Those floors became our retreat too. At home, the others of us had brothers or sisters and parents, pets, and troops of neighborhood kids and cousins, or Malcolm's Uncle Abraham above the garage, or Kip's mother's chattery friends at the kitchen table, or Henry's mother's piano students pounding away. But Rupert could ascend to quiet, room after room and even a winding back stair to an empty fourth floor of bare wood, light and dust. His aunt kept the furnace belching from September to May, hot gusts sweeping up the wide front staircase to Rupert's silent domain.

Up there you came upon even more mahogany and oak, high, thick, purposeless as if in a museum — the lavish compensation from his aunt's former employers, the Tavistocks, who'd settled her in this closed-up town house of some long dead relative of theirs. She had, after all, shepherded the Tavistocks' two sons and their daughter for twenty-five years.

You wouldn't have liked Aunt Undine anyway, Anna. She has stood against every door you opened for us, as if to keep her Rupert from passing through with the rest of us. Yes, she's alive, and still Rupert goes to her nursing home to let her stare at him, silently, for an hour each week. When he's leaving she may manage to say, "Never should I have left home, Rupert," or "Never, never should I have come here to this place." Is "this place" America, Rupert still wonders, or the Tunxet Brook Home? The Tavistock sons keep an eye on her too and supplement her monthly pension when necessary.

Amazingly, Anna, we are now ourselves nearing the age of Rupert's aunt back when she began her long disintegration. We are all together here, passing ten days' time on a far island whose rocky hips rise from the sea. We are forty-three years old, the age you were when we ourselves were born. If you had lived, we would be half your age by now. We're slowly catching up to you.

IT WAS on the wide scuffed floorboards at the top of Rupert's house that we gathered, the four of us, for the first time ever outside of school. The windows were open because it was early September. We were sixteen, and we had just been chosen by you. You wanted us to stay an extra hour after school, twice a week, for our last two years at Quissick High, simply for the love of it. We barely knew you. None of us took your Spanish because we all took French; back then Spanish was for the slower students (Kip's brother Cato in ninth grade had you, and you had him hating you already). But you'd read some of Malcolm's populist diatribes in the *Quorum*; you'd read Kip's beatnik poetry in the *Quiddity*; you'd become aware of Henry when he sang an aria from *Faust* at the Spring Sing — *Some talent is there, child,* you said to coax him in your direction; and Rupert had been so noticeably unkempt through tenth grade in your study hall, where you couldn't help but watch him as he dreamed his way through one moldy volume of Dickens after another — you'd wanted to take and bathe him and dress him up properly, you told us, and make him sit straight *um Gottes Willen!* You scared us, Anna, the way you scared everybody else. Aylmer doesn't let anyone off easy; that was the word in the corridors of QHS.

So we were sitting where the sunlight of Rupert's attic windows cut across the floorboards, and we were speculating: What are we in for now? "It'll look good applying for college," Malcolm said. "If we survive her, that is."

As we found ourselves newly cast as a quartet, Malcolm seemed our likely leader. He was — is still — wise looking, with high forehead and sharp cheekbones and eyes turning fierce whenever he concentrates hard. He had a particular standing because the Phippses were old Yankees, the remnant of a clan that began lighting out for the West a century and a half ago, leaving their more timid cousins behind. Everyone knew their aged house, an unadorned colonial just a block from school; Malcolm Phipps was the only one of us you chose who knew the other three already.

He had a history of attaching himself to a best friend. As boys, he and Kip Skerritt had done everything together — ridden bikes, played with model cars, put out a neighborhood newspaper — until Kip was assigned to North for middle school. Malcolm stayed at South and fell in with Henry Vigneault when he was elected student council treasurer during Henry's presidency. Then at Quissick High, with Henry newly involved in his singing, Malcolm befriended scrawny Rupert Eid, with his tangled mess of curls and ankles bared by socks that wouldn't stay up, and for the first time Malcolm Phipps had a best friend less generally admired than himself. "All right, Vigneault," he'd tried explaining to Henry, "so you probably wouldn't like this Rupert kid either. My mother wonders what I'm doing with a friend from Plashing Falls at all. Us sorts of guys would never even go there except biking through over to the ponds. But I've got to get to know the world, Vigneault, if I'm going into journalism. Rupert knows a whole different side of things. He isn't protected like we are." Henry, never one to feel slighted, was glad Malcolm was becoming more adventurous.

But Kip, who had been expecting high school would revive their old friendship, was more bothered by this insinuating Rupert. "You and I go all the way back to kindergarten, Skerritt," Malcolm reassured him. "You're more literary now and I'm more political. It happens. The more you learn, the more you end up different. But no one will ever know me as well as you do." "How come," said Kip, "you won't try reading Kerouac even though I'm on to him but now you're suddenly reading that big fat Dickens all because of this Rupert Eid?" Actually, Malcolm was stuck a hundred pages into *Bleak House* and never got any further. But it wasn't so much the reading of the books; what appealed to him was the idea of the volumes themselves, which had come along with the town house Rupert had moved into with his aunt when she stopped working for the Tavistocks, shelves and shelves of sets of books beneath brownish old prints on all the walls and dust everywhere. "But, Skerritt," said Malcolm, "it's not as though I can't have more than one friend." And so the first two high school years Malcolm tried to keep his friends in careful equilibrium, but apart. You, however, must have sensed our elusive connection, Anna, because you selected us, each one, then drew together our separate threads.

In the warm September weather, there was something soft and worn and calm about being up on Rupert's top floor, the four of us, even if Kip was still a bit cool to this Rupert, even if Henry was overeager, asking Rupert a lot of questions about his life with the Tavistocks. Tavistock was such a powerful name in the Quissick of our childhoods. It stood in story-high letters, black paint edged in white, on the red bricks below the granite crown of their warehouse in the Riverbend section of town.

But at last the talk turned to you, Anna.

What did any of us really know about you? Rumor said that you'd been married twice before you married Mr. Aylmer, that you'd left your own children behind, in Germany or maybe in Spain, that you'd been in the Spanish Civil War (on one side or the other) and then come over. But why here? You'd stayed on in Quissick all those years. We worked ourselves up imagining you might have come as some emissary from the great outside world — to us four alone, to choose us, to lead us on to our own real lives beyond the valley of the Quidnapunxet.

Imagine us then: sixteen-year-olds, soft skinned, caught when you wanted us most. You might have chosen a girl or two, but no, you said, they didn't interest you, there was Mr. Davenport for the bookish girls — he did better by them.

Here we are in your classroom: straight ahead of you, Malcolm Phipps, legs crossed tight at the knees, foot wrapped around calf but still tapping at the air, corduroys bunched up, bright plaid collar and cuffs creeping out of autumnal argyle sweater; Clifford Skerritt to one side of Malcolm, emulating a current idol with short sleeves rolled high, engineer boots firmly planted, piled paperbacks spilling off his lap — later they'd actually prohibit jeans at QHS, Anna, but this is still your time, before jeans came to stand for so much rebellion; on Malcolm's other side, Rupert Eid, notebook forgotten at home, pencil tips broken, shoes untied and scuffy, gray windbreaker, shirt untucked, eyes dreamily scanning the wall maps of Europe 1914, Europe 1938; and beyond Rupert, bright-toothed Henry Vigneault (*Vig-no* in Quissick French), legs stretched out in khakis, sweatsocks and loafers, pink shirt, golden ring, hair slicked, just beyond your easy glances, Anna, not as likely to be questioned. So you went after him.

*Yes but you must never let yourself be only so charming, Monsieur Vigneault. This is dangerous, your smile. Do you know? It is this American smile I have always to watch out for. The soil must breed it here, in Québecois, Irishman, whomever. Years and years in this country and I haven't understood it quite. Tell me, children, why do they smile so at me and then turn their backs? Oh yes, Henri, your mother has invited me to come up to the Ridge. I must see her new home, she says, and what a view she has, isn't it? After you sang last spring and I merely wanted to tell you something about your singing, and about* Faust, *the real* Faust, *maybe, so that you should know more of what you sing, and up comes Maman with such smiles. Children, am I the first person to speak to you so about your parents?*

How did Henry answer? We all only remember being silent at first.

*Now take these, one each,* Don Carlos *of Schiller, even if in English only. Read, next week, and then we will begin all over. But to really read! Not as you read for Mr. Davenport, you catch?*

Those four boys set aside from the rest, those four who'd worked very hard all their school lives, or in Rupert's case perhaps not hard but in potent bursts — they all stared back across your book-strewn desk at you, their gray sybil. What were you seeing inside them?

Take those same four, your new ones, so nervous under your darting eyes, and release them through the tumult of the hallways to the heavy doors out onto School Street and watch them awkwardly reach a decision to go, no, not by Phipps's a block away, not up Opossum Hill to Skerritt's nor all the way up the Ridge to Vigneault's, but the longer downhill walk toward Plashing Falls to confer in undisturbed quiet, with Rupert not leading the way but dragging after, as if he didn't know or care where they were all going and he was only tagging along because he didn't have a better place to go.

A twenty-minute saunter — then Malcolm is stepping up to a double door, its brass plate engraved with a meaningless HUTCHINS, goblets and pear trees etched in its frosted glass all white in the white of afternoon sun. Henry and Kip flank the steps waiting for Rupert to find his key in that wad of handkerchief in his tight pocket; his aunt hadn't bought him new pants since eighth grade. "Maybe that's why he doesn't hardly eat, so as not to outgrow his only pair," Malcolm says from his high perch. Rupert keeps searching and only faintly smiles.

And then we're safely past snoring Aunt Undine and up a flight of stairs splendid enough, Anna, that its railing, its newel post and balusters were salvaged when the house was later subdivided. Then up again, past a tiny bay window of red and yellow glass — cherries spilling from cornucopias (future salvage too) — and on the third floor we get glimpses of yet more rockers, bedsteads, armoires, glass-fronted bookcases, dressing tables, doubtless all of Quissick manufacture a century ago, filling the rooms. But which does Rupert inhabit? He doesn't point it out — Malcolm is leading us anyway — and all the beds look utterly unrumpled. Then finally up the servants' stairs to the empty attic — here we begin to feel at ease, all of us, far above town and street, insulated by the floors below so muffled in their flowered carpets and heavy velvet curtains. Here, in sunniness, with a view out to the shadowy lump of Tunxet Mountain and those glimmers from the Quisquabaug Ponds, and to the right, closer by, the red hulks of warehouses at the bend in the river, here we find we belong together.

You knew, Anna, how high school boys learn to love each other in groups, a love they call, safely, team spirit. You imagined what strength of purpose the bookish ones might give each other when you had teamed them too.

It was daughters you left behind in Europe, wasn't it, Anna? Did they not interest you any more than our classmates in skirts did? Why did you have such an uncomfortable time with the girls? We wonder how you'd be with them today, Anna. We warn you, they aren't like they used to be. They have become more like you, in some sense. But we're not sure that would please you.

Rupert opened a window, the one thing he did that made it seem like his own house, then he sat down again, pulled off his shoes, his floppy socks, stretched his toes and scratched his soles and wrapped his arms around his knees. Finally he spoke: "My aunt doesn't want anyone ever coming over here. But I'm going to tell her. None of you's going to steal anything. You're all rich kids. She's going to get used to it in a while. So what if she yells at me?"

And so we had begun. You had already, in one hour, driven us to need to talk together. For Rupert it was soon a spilling out of things he had never yet said in his sixteen years. For Malcolm it was a consolidation of the separate talk of his private friendships. He was surrounded now by three comrades, but no longer his alone.

There was too much to say. Having always been taught so somberly, Anna, we had now discovered your light. And at school in that heavy warming west-windowed sun, even after the halls had emptied, we'd still be arguing, laughing, and then later, we four without you, walking Quissick streets, ending up at one house or another but often by sunset at Rupert's on that top floor, as on the first afternoon, or even up the ladder through the hatch to his roof, the whole town awhir around us.

"Is she crazy?" "*Don Carlos* by Tuesday?" "With everything else we're supposed to do?"

But we tried some out loud. Kip and Henry (Carlos and Posa) shouting to each other — real Schiller, the old-fashioned thing, nothing like our own modest lives. "And is it truly thou? I press thee to my bosom, and I feel thy throbbing heart beat wildly 'gainst mine own. And now all's well again."

Oh Anna, what if this has all been lost and in this new age your great Unreality is being nudged into some quiet corner? *Don Carlos?* Kip has actually tried it on his students at Quissick State. Kerouac too! Yes, Kerouac, Anna, whose windy outpourings you couldn't stomach — Kerouac and Schiller, no longer so far from each other as both from everything in this unsympathetic new world of ours. *But don't be so desperate, children,* you'll say and grab at our wrists in reassurance. *Time comes round again. I have seen it, dear ones. Nothing true is ever lost.*

We always did believe you, Anna.

Let us show you where we are now. We're still in the sun. A blossom-laden breeze cools us, and every half minute a wave makes a tremendous pounding below the cliff. That sea there is the roughest passage in the whole Caribbean. Columbus himself sailed past, naming this island but not attempting to set foot here. It's winter up in cold Massachusetts, with snow on your grave most likely, but we've escaped. We are four nearly naked men, in our forty-fourth years, reading in this sun, talking, scribbling, contemplating you same as ever, Anna. You'd recognize us instantly. We've hardly even begun to gray: Henry a little at the temples; Rupert an occasional gray wisp entangled in his brown mop; Malcolm grayer on his chest than head really, his forehead a bit higher now; Kip is nearsighted but tanned dark as he always was in any Quissick summer. He's the one under the straw hat. Rupert stretches out, still terribly thin, on the towel beside him. There are lotions we pass around in bottles numbered 10, 15, 20, supposed to shield us from a nakeder sun than the one you knew.

There's a custom down here. They set a jumbie table, as they call it, for departed spirits to partake of the Christmas feast while the living are off at church. Will you be our honorary jumbie, Anna? We'll set a place for you this Christmas Day. We know it's a long way in time and space, but we're calling to you, with the voice you heard in us all, hoping to feel you near again, Anna, teaching us, and leading us into the unknown. It gets so very dark at night here. A volcano rises behind us, the wide sea rolls, and our bungalow peeks out from a grove of palms. At night we snap out the light and look up at black fronds sweeping between us and the bright stars.

There was one hazier Massachusetts night when we were just starting up with you, still on *Don Carlos*. We were all on Rupert's roof, late. If Aunt Undine had awakened downstairs in her high four-poster, she would have presumed we'd crept out hours ago. But Rupert was telling his story, all at once now instead of in pieces, and we'd bundled up, close, under the faint stars. Kip had dared to ask him what his mother was like, as if Rupert might call up her ghost for us from across the ocean, across the years, from the last days of the terrible war during which we'd all been born.

"A whole wall fell in on her," Rupert reported as if he could remember it firsthand. "I was on the other side of the room. I'm sure I didn't stop screaming for a long time. My father was already dead in Russia, so whoever it was we lived near must've kept me safe. After the war, the Tavistocks sent Aunt Undine over to get her orphan nephew. I remember the green of the Tavistocks' farm and wet grass on my toes when I was little. Well, they called it a farm because they had cows before the war, and they still had horses at least and chickens and big vegetable gardens. That was my only world. There weren't any pictures of my mother. Aunt Undine didn't know anything about her; all she knew was that Sintram Eid, her brother, had married some girl. Maybe I'm not even her nephew. Maybe they found this baby and found somewhere else in the rubble an old letter to Sintram Eid from his sister who was a nursemaid in America. See, I could be anyone. There wasn't anything left of my mother at all. Aunt Undine says her name was supposedly Angelika — not Angelica, but in German, *Ahn-gay-lee-ka*, with a *k* not a *c*. Aunt Undine didn't know anything else about her."

"Couldn't you get your birth certificate from Germany now?" Malcolm wondered.

"She wouldn't want me to find all that out. She wouldn't want anyone coming over here and taking me from her. My father should've come to America when Aunt Undine wanted him to, but he told her he thought things were finally looking up, with Hitler in there."

"Creepy," said Henry.

"I was a little Nazi baby, see," said Rupert, smiling in the ghost white light of midnight on his Plashing Falls rooftop.

"But your mother —" Kip tried again.

"Well, what could she have been like?" said Rupert. "Some washerwoman's daughter in some back street in Cologne and married to a soldier. Was that it? There's only one thing I can ever really know for sure about her."

"What's that?" Kip said, gently.

"That she must have looked something like me."

In such pale light, with the collar of his gray windbreaker turned up, he suddenly took on the look of a German girl, curly head, bright eyes, small nose, smooth cheeks. He felt it, the others saw it. His own mother emerged from his face for a moment, visited us — we saw her, felt her — and then Rupert's lips turned down, the brightness left his eyes, and she was gone.

That night he told how his real name was Ruprecht but his Aunt Undine had changed it so he'd fit in better here. The Tavistocks were proud of themselves for bringing him over. By the time Rupert could remember, he had their farm mostly to himself, with the Tavistock kids at boarding schools. He ran around the fields and climbed the trees, a country boy who hadn't seen a city even as large as Quissick since his first two lost years in Germany.

Rupert told how once, rocking on the porch swing when he was ten, probably, he half-heard Mrs. Tavistock inside laughing with her husband. She was remembering all the Tavistock dogs and all the people who'd worked for the Tavistocks over the years and all the stories about them. And then Rupert heard, through the window open behind his head, her saying how funny Undine was, how funny her English was, how she called hydrangeas "hygeraniums" and Yorkshire pudding "Yorkster pudding" and how she said the news from Europe was "heart-rendering." The Tavistocks were howling in laughter.

Henry proposed we all drive out and see the Tavistock place for ourselves the next day. We imagined piling into the cab of one of the Vigneault Lumber Company trucks and taking off, us four together. But David Tavistock had taken over the farm by then and Rupert wasn't sure if we should.

To us Quissick boys, most places still seemed far from each other. Even Plashing Falls seemed a place far from Opossum Hill or Parapet Ridge, so to drive out the Leominster Road half an hour seemed too significant an exploration. Even you, Anna, you'd settled into Quissick leaving a whole old world behind; and when you told us of going to theaters and concerts, you meant decades ago on another continent. That was music for you still, and drama, back then, there, far away. *Separated from it by a horror, dear ones. I never think back to the innocent time without some shudder, you know, passing through my breast to remind me of what has come in between.*

But what did our Quissick offer you then, Anna? For us, it seemed big enough. How much space did we need for reading books, for taking walks or biking, for looking up at stars? How much space did we need for becoming friends for life?

But for you, Anna?

After you died, Quissick got smaller in our minds, and soon enough it was too small even for us. True, it went about emptying itself out for quite a while, and it became much poorer. But of late it's begun filling up once more, and you wouldn't recognize it. Kip lives in town again, and Rupert can be found just outside, where the hog farms used to be. We, all four, come and go easily again. And look at us way down here on our veranda among palms, on an island perhaps you never heard of. It might have been a country of its own, but it's only a colony still, one of the last remaining, hesitant (because it's so small) to cut itself adrift from the Old World. Yet over a hundred other nations have come into being since we four were born. We have seen history now too.

THANK YOU, once, now and forever, for giving us to each other — and in your particular way. Had you never picked us out, made us talk to you, we might have been off in different directions all too soon. Think of Kip, the searcher after what have come to be called role models (there are so many phrases to teach you, Anna). The dead James Dean, the fictional Dean Moriarty or (in a different mood) a hipster comic he'd heard on a record called Lord Buckley — not that Kip behaved like any of these, but he did work at a certain aura, to mask his connection to daily life under the sagging eaves of the huge creaky Skerritt house on Opossum Hill, where too large a family, with too many chattering visitors and wide-open doors and windows and hollerings back and forth, made him yearn to be like someone else instead.

You'll be pleased to know he's Clifford Skerritt now to most of the rest of the world — the "Kip" annoyed you so. But in Skerritt manner, Clifford was always Kip, Kenneth was Cato, Eileen Io, the next ones somehow kept Connel and Coral (nicknames already, in effect), but finally came

Oops, who was really Elizabeth. You recall that pack, Anna? Now we can confess to you something shameful and cruel: it was Cato Skerritt and his bad pals from Upper Quiddy who lowered that flag from the classroom window above yours. We four sat, thinking at first a cloud had passed over the sun, but your face, Anna . . . It was the Nazi flag Mr. Skerritt had brought back from the war, and it belonged in a trunk in their attic with the leavings of every other era in Skerritt history. In third grade, Kip had shown it secretly to his best friend Malcolm Phipps, and there was something tangibly awful about it even then, its tiny moth holes, its brilliant redness. And yet a decade later, Cato could pick it up without a qualm, sneak it off to QHS and lower it slowly over that west window. As soon as we turned, Kip and Malcolm knew, but they didn't tell you, Anna, none of us ever told you. We tried to act puzzled too.

That's what you'd do, Anna Aylmer, when a thing really troubled you: express puzzlement. Oh, when you were mistress of the situation, you could produce any amount of outrage: *But* Moby-Dick, *children! What has he in his mind? That he should teach* Moby-Dick *to tenth graders — ach, the great Mr. Davenport, he is such a teacher, dear ones. Listen only to the parents: Mr. Davenport this, Mr. Davenport that.* And we'd chuckle along, wonder-filled at our alliance with you. But whenever something made no sense and you went somehow blank (your face, Anna, when we thought merely a cloud had passed), then all you could say was *But what is it, I don't quite see, c'était très étrange, children,* and then luckily the sun suddenly came back. Anna, you couldn't ever say: They're doing this because they mistake who I am, because for them a certain accent, a certain origin can mean one thing only. Or instead perhaps: They hate me for my study halls, they know this flag is my nightmare, they're tormenting me.

You wouldn't have a "they" in your life. You were not like Aunt Undine, now in Tunxet Brook imagining "them" (Communists? Tavistocks?) bedeviling her still. She keeps flicking at motes on her shoulders, twitching her head to catch sight of them, brushing at them to get them off — "Verdammt!" But as for you, Anna, what we can surely see at last is that you were more afraid in this unsympathetic world than we ever realized then, where all we could tell you was: "Mrs. Aylmer, it's just a prank. This school's full of jerks. Kids think something like that's a laugh riot." *But what, children? I didn't catch.*

That night at home Kip beat up on Cato. Kip wasn't inclined to violence, despite his engineer boots and leather bomber jacket. But that night he and Cato crashed and banged all over their third floor. Kip slammed him at the pressboard wall separating their bedrooms and bashed it right through. A lamp toppled, a bulb smashed, a chair leg broke off, Cato's bed frame practically collapsed. It was an all-out wrestle such as two brothers alone are capable of. Io came screaming from her room. Mr. Skerritt bellowed from the first floor, too absorbed in the *Quotidian* to budge, so finally it was Mrs. Skerritt, pounding upstairs with Oops clinging to her elbow, who screeched loud enough to break through the murderousness. The boys did penance for weeks. Neither would tell what the fight was about, neither would blame the other, so for a month they both had to perform all the family chores — raking, dish-washing, floor waxing, repainting porch railings, cleaning out the back of the garage, rebuilding the bedroom wall. After dinner, Io would lean back and gloat: "You may take my plate now, slaves." Her brothers endured silently till December first; then Cato went back to hanging out with the bad influences from Upper Quiddy, and Kip holed up in his room with Kerouac's *Maggie Cassidy* and *Doctor Sax*.

All over that flag, Anna, and rightly — but no, all over you, really. Why, when you had us so scared, did we feel we were the ones who had to protect you? Why did we feel you saw us, four American teenagers, as your refuge? Weren't we presuming too much, Mrs. Aylmer?

But somber moments on those afternoons with you still resonate in our heads. Your explication of a poem: *There is an ember still barely glowing. It is the memory of the last breath of a life. And only love can stir it up, dear ones, make it grow again warm.* "Requiem" by Friedrich Hebbel, you made us fathom it — remember that particular hour, Anna? Your final version: *Soul, forget not the Dead. See how they hover round you, shivering, forsaken. But if, growing cold, you were to close yourself off from them, they would be seized in the storm of night . . .* And then came difficult lines we couldn't get. You gave us the German poem; you told us what each word, in itself, meant; you explained case endings and genders, but it was puzzling, Anna, even for Rupert, whose more domestic boyhood version of the language was fast leaving him.

*But I must teach you translation, dear ones. That is the key to literature, when you can hear something one way*

*and know to say it in your own words another.* "Dem
sie, zusammengekrampft in sich, trotzten im Schosse
der Liebe . . ." Zusammengekrampft — some word, Anna!
*Tightly indrawn,* you finally put it. And upon the lap of
love — no, within the bosom of love, we guessed, maybe
even within love's womb, tightly indrawn, they — those
embers — might defy that night storm . . .

We are in mourning, Anna, again, the four of us, and
that is why we find ourselves turning back especially to
you, our teacher. At the memorial service for our friend,
Henry was determined to sing that old poem of ours, in
the setting for baritone by Max Reger. "Seele, vergiss sie
nicht, Seele, vergiss nicht die Todten." His voice soared
above the grieving heads, and we other three heard your
voice too, inside his. *Soul, forget not the Dead.*

It was you, after all, who taught us to sense voices
within voices. During that class, Anna, a fading afternoon hour in November, we heard something underneath
yours — a plea. That afternoon you yourself became
like glowing embers to us, "die den Armen die Liebe
schürt" — *embers that love alone rakes up for the poor.*
Hard to phrase it: you rake embers to keep them aglow,
the poor have no one to do the raking for them, but love —
we could only make it sound crass in English. You had us
feeling it, though, even if we didn't find elegant phrases.
What was it that made the words you put before us seem
like they were, at that instant, you, Anna? You became
words. We've never been the same again.

Envisioning that poem scratched across the blackboard, then translated, lines here, lines there, crossed out,
emended in crumbling chalk, it's as if we're seeing you

tremulously before us, enjoining us to attend to something large and old, a huge past, volumes full of language, because if we forget, we will have ceased loving, and only our love can rake those dying embers. How's that? Have we caught it? Because you were our poor, weren't you, Anna? A voice deeper than your audible voice was telling us — we're sure now — *I'm poor, children, I live alone in a foreign town, I speak with a heavy accent, I drive a rusty 1939 Plymouth coupe, I have two small rooms in the Riverbend section among warehouses by the train yards, I teach in a grim granite high school unappreciated, I have no family, no friends here because I am a difficult old woman and don't understand you smiling Americans . . .* "Señora Aylmer, won't you come visit us up on the Ridge, let us have you for dinner? We're house-proud, I admit, we're eager to show off our view. It's the newest colonial with the veranda, you can see it up above Cross Street. You know, I got Henry started on the piano when we lived in Tunxet Farms, but voice is his real love. Aren't I a lucky mother?"

The voices, Anna, that you made us hear, voices inside and outside, such voices as we'd taken to be merely our mothers' and fathers' or aunt's or uncle's, you made us hear them afresh. Who'd ever spoken of our families in such a way? Who'd ever mocked them? We were only virginal boys, secretive still in our desires, zusammengekrampft (how's that?) in our passions, American boys trained in the school of Mr. Davenport. *Ach, Mr. Davenport — he imagines they will have fun with the whaling. But he is more suited to the girls, dear ones.* You got us conspiring to make you feel you were the only one who could really see, or hear, or teach us.

And yet you were also, somehow, our poor.

We see your rattling Plymouth chugging you along Quissick streets, encountering us once at the corner of School and Bridge on our way over to Rupert's. You didn't notice at first: you were looking straight ahead, blinking in the setting sunlight, but your quick right turn nearly mowed us down. Rupert leapt up on the fender howling in pain, leather-jacketed Kip played cop, Henry a crank bystander. "She's crazy, Officer, she drives like a crazy lady!" Poor Anna, your face, not sure of the joke, looking to Malcolm for rescue, but Rupert was in stitches already and Malcolm couldn't think fast enough of a role to assume, so in a matter of ten seconds the playlet was over and we stood there, amazed at ourselves for having ribbed you so. *Oh mes enfants, mes enfants* was all you could say — French, your language in embarrassing moments.

Then we watched you chug off alone down Bridge Street toward looming Riverbend, where no one lived at all. (Some of those warehouses are being turned into condos now, Anna. *What are condos, children?*) Back then there were only the dark red hulks, to which trudged workers, from Lower and Upper Quiddy and from Tunxet Village across the river, along misty early morning streets and back again along the sun-flooded streets of afternoon, the opposite direction from four book-laden high school boys. "Look at these little queers!" a bulky man once growled at us, bumping hard into Henry's shoulder as stifled laughter richocheted behind us. We didn't look around. We never told you that particular story, Anna. We didn't even remind each other of it till some years after your death.

So much to remind ourselves of, so much to tell you.

Anna the Jumbie, are you on your way to join our feast

at Christmas? As local lore has it, we will not be permit-
ted to greet you, for we must be off at church, leaving the
table piled high, and then you will sweep in, unheard, unseen, to devour our mortal food. Don't be afraid of the island jumbies, Anna, they won't find you strange. You are
all the dead now, one great family. We've learned to cook
breadfruit here, so you'll eat the same as them. But of
course, we won't actually be off at church; we'll be seeking
a more pagan communion, motoring the precipitous island roads. We'll drive up to the mouth of the volcano and
down to lava black beaches, or wander goat-dotted valleys
in the long grass. And we'll imagine you sitting back here
in our bungalow, reading our thoughts, discovering what
has become of us.

Could it possibly still matter to you, Anna? The vanity
of students, who think every teacher will be passionately
interested in their achievements forevermore — Professor
Skerritt corroborates that it gets awfully tiresome. But
here we are, still expecting your attention, Anna, because
you left us before we had grown away from you at all, before we could see you going on in a world with new students, without us.

Will you come all this way from a Quissick graveyard?
You must be prepared to find it a poor country. Tour-
ists aren't much attracted to its black sand pounded by
such violent surf. Hurricanes have destroyed all the lime
groves. People born here are leaving. As many islanders
live now up in Massachusetts as live in the village where
we buy our bread and beer and fruit. It was, in fact, one of
Kip's colleagues at Quissick State who rented us his own
bungalow here, a peaceful place to abide a period of uncer-

tainty, to soothe ourselves in private limbo while back at home Professor Howard prepares his lectures on Third World Anglophone literature for next term. Two nights ago, we four — would-be islanders — were to be seen stepping along behind a slow-moving flatbed truck that bore a heavily amplified soca band. Hundreds of people were out for the big jump-up — the gentle old calypso is gone. But we won't become nostalgic over someone else's fading culture. We'll leave that to Kip's colleague, who has a right to it.

What would you make of your untraveled Quissick boys down here in the Third World? *Third World I hear you say again, children. But how many worlds are there?* It's festival time. Don't you want to join us? Please, Anna, we miss you. We have missed you twenty-five years.

**B**UT AM I crazy? I said by Tuesday, dear ones, not Thursday. Here I have it written. And so no one has read the García Lorca? But this is terrible. Why are we here, why do I give you this time? This is your time, muchachos, it is not my time. I have no time. What time does a teacher possibly have, surrounded with children who do not consider maybe the world is not made for them and teachers are not made for them? You are bottle-fed Americans, my little ones . . . "Not me," spoke up Rupert. You turned on him. He couldn't help saying it, and now he sat shaking under your eyes, the gray collar of his windbreaker up against his skinny neck, drumming alternately thumb and small fingers very fast against his thigh. Not you? No, not you. No, you are different, Herr Ruprecht Eid. That is for sure, you are different. You do not even know how to excuse yourself like these nice polite American boys. You see, they explain how they had to practice for Christmas recital, or Mother made them wax floors, or the troublesome uncle above the garage forgot his sedative, isn't it? But I do not hear excuse from you,

*Herr Eid. You look up and say, "Not me." Well. And am I never to say not me? May I not be allowed, I, the teacher? Let me try it: Not me! And now I go. Good afternoon, muchachos.* Exit Mrs. Aylmer.

You were awful to us.

We sat in our row, then Henry began to laugh, and that made us all itchier. Then he couldn't quite stop. "Henry!" said Malcolm, grabbing him by both cheeks and squeezing, turning his lips into fish lips. The laughter kept spurting. "Stop it, Henry." But he couldn't. Kip tried calming him, arm around shoulder, a steadying pat. "Breathe regular, in then out, look at the maps, look at all the green of France — those are fields — and the white cool Alps . . ." Finally, Henry stopped.

"I was saying 'not me' about bottle feeding," Rupert had tried to explain between Henry's fits. "I wasn't saying 'not me' about being American. I'm American. What else am I? She's crazy. She asks us if she's crazy, and we're supposed to say no of course not. But she is crazy. All those old women from over there are crazy. Can you imagine a continent full of crazy women?" Henry burst out again, spurts of trembling laughter. We set out walking him up Parapet Ridge, thinking he'd better get home.

His house was strange to the three of us who didn't live there, who lived instead in creaky old houses with window frames that rattled and peeling plaster where there'd been leaks, but Henry was accustomed to this newness. The Vigneaults used to live across the river in Tunxet Farms, that apple-and-pear-orchard-turned-suburb for which you, Anna, had the greatest scorn. *Tunxet Farms, that is the goal of civilization, dearest ones, so I am told.* Nonetheless, pampered Henry was brought up with windows tightly fitting, with no stairs to climb, with a garage door that pulled up electrically, a kitchen all built in and no bare floors to be seen, so he didn't feel so coddled by the splendid new house on the Ridge as the rest of us did. Whenever we visited, Mrs. Vigneault pressed on us after-school treats of ice cream with pineapple chunks and strawberry jam and chocolate sauce.

"Henry's got hiccups or something," Malcolm told her now. "He can't stop."

Henry's mom squeezed him tight, pulling him to the kitchen yelling back to her piano student, "Betty, now play the sonatine." Henry had to bend over, hold a long glass of apple juice in his fingers while his thumbs pinched his nose, and drink from the opposite rim upside down. Bleary-eyed Henry raised his head to us and grinned without a hint of a lurking giggle.

We four stepped out onto the veranda in the cold December wind, and there beneath us was Quissick. "I feel naked up here," said Malcolm. There was the severe-looking Phipps house below us, and there on squat Opossum Hill to the north were the Skerritts' elaborate gables. The great edifice of Quissick High School stood between them, and behind the hill the business blocks on Common and Market lined up as a sort of immobile freight train. Turning west, we saw the indistinguishable flat roofs of Plashing Falls, one of them Rupert's, then came a gap where the Quidnapunxet must have been flowing icily, and on the other bank Henry's previous suburban neighborhood bristling with skinny bare trees. (Those maples and oaks have grown tall now, Anna; it has begun to seem pleasant and even old-fashioned in Tunxet Farms.)

"My forebears," Malcolm went on, "would never have thought of settling up here. The Parapet was for climbing to and for quarrying out behind, never for living on. Leave it to Canucks to move up here." Henry tackled Malcolm and twisted him dangerously close to the railing. "And who was so stupid as to sell this ridge off? Yankees, eh? And now who's getting rich in construction, Phipps?"

Then calmly, leaning against the railing as the sun set behind Tunxet Mountain, Henry tried to explain your effect on him, Anna. "She has me on edge so. It just started happening. What kind of big horrible mother is she trying to be? That's not the mother I'm used to, guys. I've had it. I've got enough work to do with my singing. Can't I get out of it?"

Rupert was sitting on the redwood planks, back against the railing, staring at the setting sun that glared off the windowpanes. Kip reached his arm around Henry for the second time that afternoon. "But you can't leave us with her alone, Vigneault. It's got to be the four of us. She'd try to make us turn on you. 'Maybe he has no real feeling for music after all, children.'" "You're blackmailing me," Henry said. Malcolm's eyes watched sadly over the broad valley.

But Christmas season had come, so our hours with you were preempted anyway by exams and rehearsals. And we thought of you, alone in your two rooms over the luncheonette, watching snow softly cover the train yards. You put off your dinner at the Vigneaults'. You sank back uninterruptedly into your reading. You didn't bother to shovel out your old coupe for the two weeks of vacation, but Rupert saw your light on up there, saw your broad shape once in the window when he went roaming one dark night on the way home from Kip's.

Were you already planning that we four would see you out of your life, Anna? Even then, was there no chance we might do well enough by you to cause a change in your direction? You had become obsessed with us, hadn't you? We felt it. We took up so much of your thought in your last years. Even at that early point, after Henry's laughing fit, December of eleventh grade, you had so engaged yourself with us that the slightest disappointment could enrage you. *But am I crazy?* Moment of reversal. *Well, let me try it: Not me! There. And now I go.*

We all might have decided to stop subjecting ourselves to you. On Henry's veranda we seemed to hover over our safe childhoods down below us. Rupert, his back to the wind, never dressed warmly enough, but Kip liked the blast in his face and let his black hair blow wild. Malcolm was saying, "This is a decisive moment in our lives. We could choose. I think we all have something to learn. Why does she do this to us? But then who else is there like her? Don't we really have to stay?"

Anna, now you know how we talked of abandoning you.

But after Christmas, when you were so glad to see us again and you hugged us one by one, *dear ones, dearest ones,* and you had forgotten about the García Lorca confusion — then we came to realize it was because you had been in Spain when Lorca was killed, that you must have been planning how you'd lead us back into that moment in your history, through Lorca, but we had misunderstood the deadline, we had been mere undiscerning boys just when your soul was eager for communion. We're so sorry,

Anna. Had you hoped to start telling us of the hells you'd been through?

*All stories are about time.* You did tell us that. Your time? *I have no time.* And so where are we now? Hovering over our time too, like you, finally, Anna, in a moment of reversal? Look at us here in the hot sun. Where are the marks of time on our four healthy-looking browning bodies? Do we still think as acutely, do we listen, do we hear? You did teach us those things, whatever pain we may have caused you. So young on that other veranda in the cold: were there already the first marks of time in Malcolm's hand-shaded eyes pondering Quissick, in Kip's wild hair, in Rupert's knees huddled and shivering? Or in Henry's deepening, broadening tones as he launched his *Faust* aria —"Avant de quitter ces lieux"— into the wind.

ALREADY our first spring with you, Anna, you had begun striking us with evidence of the workings of time. You made us look ourselves over and take note. "I must have been changing a lot this year," Henry wrote in one of those free papers you kept squeezing out of us, "or maybe I just became more sure of myself. But staring out at three hundred people from the stage of the Valley Theater last Friday night, I felt I became a different person." *I felt I had become, I felt I had become a different person, child. Do I teach you your own language? Yes, Heinrich, and so?* We were used to your interruptions.

"Now I know what I want to do with my life," Henry went on, reading his paper aloud on a sleety April afternoon. Across your desk you almost smiled, Anna, a hint of your own triumph on your lips. He had written how all through childhood his mother had kept him at his music, how the piano in their living room in Tunxet Farms had seemed like a giant black bug with its wing up, and how his singing voice somehow felt free in a way his fingers never did. But he still had his insecurities: "They probably cast me," he wrote, "only so they could get a discount on lumber for the sets from my dad."

You remember how Kip protested that Henry's prose wasn't really writing at all, just talk on paper. You remember Kip's own unpunctuated evocations flooding pages of three-hole paper: "dreamangels hovering over mudblack bricks of dim sorrowful Quissick sidewalks —" Or Malcolm — you can hear him: "When one first encounters the works of . . ." You made us drop our poses, Anna. You took a look at our final papers for Mr. Davenport and declared, *But, my dearest ones, it is all so cunning. "One feels moved by the . . ." Why do you write this? Are you the Opossum Hill Ladies' Reading Circle? Basta! I have no interest in what this famous "one" feels. No, but you must do the feeling yourselves.* "Well, in college essays," Malcolm began to protest, so you stormed on: *What do we care about college essays? We are here in Quissick High School, sorrowful Quissick High School, as Comrade Skerritt would have it, and you will learn to write what lies inside you. College essays!* Malcolm would have added, "Still, Mr. Davenport . . ." but he knew better than to set you off any further. "That's so cool, Señora Aylmer," said Kip, "you and Jack Kerouac are more alike than you think." *Yes and also I am a drunken beatnik, I admit to it*, you said, mischief at the corners of your eyes.

Henry pleased you most then, didn't he, Anna? He was the first to unbosom himself that spring. All his powers were awakening: Henry the coddled late bloomer, his red-gold hair slicked back with Wildroot, his pink cheeks — he was sprouting, outstripping even Kip in a matter of months. No wonder he was cast in his first opera, as the handsome drummer boy; no wonder he found himself swept into that circle of musical and theatrical types, our little sub-Bohemia, of whom some taught at Quissick State, others led leisured lives in the surrounding countryside, and a few even bubbled up from hardworking Quissick itself. They always went for coffee after late rehearsals and earnestly attended as Ted Soteropoulos, the stage director from the college, held forth on the origins of comedy in the Dionysian fertility rite. It was only *The Gondoliers*, the Quidnapunxet Light Opera's annual spring show, but Ted, leaning closer to wide-eyed Henry in the big booth at the rear of Boyle's, had his ideas. With his meaty arm flung across the back of the booth, he would give Henry a squeeze on the far shoulder. Henry would smile and chuckle and blush a bit and feel, despite it all, somehow sophisticated amongst these artistic people.

You were instantly concerned, weren't you, Anna, about Soteropoulos. *And he is always telling you how charming you are? You see, I know the man. Child, this is theater, understand please. Once he asked if I — Anna Aylmer — would act Ibsen's Mrs. Alving in* Ghosts. *The flattery! I, who am a shy woman, an actress? But you see, one of his young protégés was to play the syphilitic son.* Ghosts, *in Quissick, even in 1950, it was a little risqué, I tell you. I declined to play it, but I wouldn't have minded setting so many tongues clacking. His protégé was quite good, I must say. But the Mrs. Alving! Well, and how does Soteropoulos costume you, Enrico, if I may know? Something with tights, I imagine.*

Anna, it's not that you were ever exactly a moralist. We

suppose you simply wanted us attuned to what you considered a worldliness beyond the ken of studious boys from a Massachusetts mill town. Subtly, you had us listen to the "Erlkönig" in our very next class. *Can you hear what it is really about, children? The seductive voice under the playful one?* A quavery falsetto emerged through the scratches on your old record — the Erl-King as tempter of the young. "I don't think Goethe had such a dirty mind," Malcolm commented crisply. *But why do you resist it so, dear one? It is there, is it not?* "But you're always being so Freudian," whined Malcolm. *And why only Freudian, my child? Did Freud invent desire? But listen to the voices in the poem, and the way Schubert has set them — the father, the child, the invisible elf. Do you not feel it? The father astride his galloping horse, his boy in his arms, and when he reaches home? The child is dead. That is all we can see. The rest is in voices. My dearest child, come go with me, such glorious games I will play with you. Isn't it?* Malcolm's brow was knotting up, his eyes tending toward each other briefly, a sign of resistance — you wouldn't leave him alone.

But Henry was opening up to you. He had, in some essence, truly changed. As he told it in his paper, it was as if he had been transformed in a single night. To the Valley audience it was merely another cheerful QLO production, with fellow citizens making themselves ridiculous but also a bit magical on the movie house stage. But when it got to the final coronation scene, Henry had started to feel a deeper delight spreading through him. There he stood, with all these older folk he'd been rehearsing with, week after week: a red velvet curtain was about to close them off from the world beyond the orchestra pit, and he would remain in some lost glowing other little world, fading from their memories but retrievable in a mere snippet of a tune whistled on an evening stroll weeks later, a world that was nicely measured off by a conductor's stick, not a clock ticking evenly through time but more irregular and surprising. Something inside Henry was letting loose, but no — that wasn't quite it; he tried very hard in his paper to re-create the exact sensation. Something was also pulling him in tight like a rope, loose and tight at once — that was it — as though the music gave him wonderful expressive freedom but still kept him in tempo. He knew everything he was expected to sing before he sang it, and then he had to make it look like he was singing it all for the first time. He would watch the conductor's beat out of the corner of his eye — do you remember how he put it, Anna? "I want to do that for all my life. I want to be tragic sometime also. I want to be heroic and then sad and then funny again, then romantic, then evil — everything! I want to be like a Schiller play, I want to let go with all I have inside but with that beat always, measured off by music, the notes and words already counted out. I know I shouldn't decide my future like this because how do I even know yet if I have a real voice? But if I do, then I know I must always make it sing." Henry closed his notebook and looked up across your desk at you.

Those free papers you scrutinized so, Anna! We drafted and redrafted and in agony awaited your verdict: *Yes, Heinrich, this is it. These are your words. There is no Davenport here. I feel you upon the stage, your own self. You bring me to my own excitement again, seeing you there, so vibrant I would say. And the lovely young woman you sang duets with, Rhonda Dewey — you know, Rhonda was one of Davenport's girls some years ago, Rhonda Calhoun now — nicht? — Rhonda Dewey Calhoun in the American fashion of entrapping the maiden name —* Always following your thought off the track, Anna, but even after the longest loop, to our amusement, you'd find your way back on: *And so it was at the dénouement, then came your greatest conviction? Yes, you have a métier, Henry, that is clear. Oh but you must not imagine Professor Soteropoulos sitting upon the summit of art. Much lies beyond Soteropoulos, I assure you. I did not hear of this Gilbert and Sullivan until I came here. Of course, it is not what they would have been giving in Berlin when I was your age. But perhaps it is a start.* Gondoliers, Gounod — *we shall be on to Wagner and Verdi in good time.*

You hadn't meant to dampen his triumph, Anna; you were merely imagining a future for him in the continental opera houses. But you noticed his reddening cheeks and added, *Ach, my child, I am perhaps still too heated in my judgments, am I not? Already I am guilty of not appreciating Monsieur Kerouac over there, and now I am finding the English opera maybe too silly for my passionate nature. I am a most opinionated old Teuton, it would seem.*

Three of us, surprised, looked across your cluttered desk into your quickly softening eyes. Then Rupert, raising his head from its usual droop, said quietly, "I don't like it when you start talking about German this and English that and French something else, Mrs. Aylmer. Can't we just read and learn and think without nations always?" "And you didn't even mention Irish," threw in Kip. But your softness was already becoming sad, your eyes turning down into your puffy cheeks, Anna, as if you had glimpsed a vision of Rupert's dangerous babyhood in the rubble of Cologne, no longer with his Angelika to shield him. *You want so much to leave old Europe behind you, don't you, mein Kind?*

Rupert had extracted a fullness of feeling from you we hadn't quite known before; your ever-present intellect seemed to vanish for an instant and you were only mother, friend. It sobered us. Was it when we, unseasoned as we were, opposed you, Anna, that we learned most to touch you? When we ourselves became impassioned, you knew you had won us over. Then you could retreat, you could drop your argument, you could put your hands flat on your desk, lean forward, capitulate, understand, bless us for the speaking of our minds.

Later, on Rupert's roof with all of springtime Quissick blowing into our nostrils, even Malcolm admitted he appreciated it that you always got so exercised. "She doesn't just analyze things to find out what the artist means, like Mr. Davenport testing us on symbolism," he explained, his nervous hands aflutter with sudden insight. "She wants us to know the art somehow from inside. It's like how at your opera, Vigneault, with all that singing and dancing going on, I kept getting a tingle in my neck. It's the same as I get sometimes when Uncle Abraham is sorting his stamps. And I get it around Aylmer a lot. I always get it when I see someone who loves what he's doing. I think Aylmer wants us to get to really know things and then just to love them. She doesn't want us to be only smart, she wants us actually to love things." The four of us sat thinking, casting long shadows across the glinting asphalt roofing. Malcolm had put it exactly as we each felt it.

But alongside this love that you were drawing from inside us, Anna, what desires (did you ever wonder?) were also welling up in each of us? You, who searched out voices underneath voices, did you ever listen for certain hidden tones in your four young dear ones, or were you shy of hearing them, Anna? *But there will be time for romances. You Americans make such a rush of it. When I was your age, oh, a student of your background, he might eventually have a little modiste, you see, someone to visit discreetly, not the sort he'd imagine marrying, oh no, but just a little modiste perhaps, who would never hope to have him all for her own.* Anna, when you were in school your Kaiser was losing a war, wasn't he? What sexual idylls were you inventing for our Prussian counterparts? Weren't they all dying by thousands? Maybe you had loved one of them, we guessed; you had already mentioned something about a first love — not one of your husbands, you made that clear — and hadn't we once heard you murmur, as if to yourself: . . . *leaving me with something most precious* — was that it? We didn't dare ask you to explain further; there were moments we knew we were merely being privileged with mysterious glimpses of a proscribed history. And so we challenged you on safer ground. Back in high school, we were appalled by your attitude on sexual relations. Girls were our friends, our comrades — Mr. Davenport's girls: Lucy Idlenot, Karla Hamell, Nellie McVinney. And try finding a self-effacing little modiste in Quissick in 1961. We had a hell of a battle with you that afternoon, didn't we, Anna?

Perhaps you were helping us to stave something off. You knew none of us had a steady date, none of us went out much at all, except occasionally in groups to a movie at the Valley. Your boys did best with passion left, for a time, safely on pages. Let life follow art, and a good deal behind, you probably thought. In a way we thank you, Anna. You didn't smirk at Henry's wanting to be heroic, pathetic, romantic; you would never snicker at us when we used words from our souls, words written or spoken or sung — because words were your element, Anna, and to an extent, because of you, ours.

But in adolescence maybe even words begin to move and tremble out of their first meanings. Surely, you saw that happening all about us, to us, too — how could it not? If you had known that Kip had taken to staying on at Rupert's after Henry and Malcolm had headed back across town, what might you have imagined? And if you had known of their lusty experiments in one or another of those massive mahogany beds? We're sure that you, Anna, would have been the least likely in Quissick to be disapproving. But if it had persisted? As it had — as it has? We wonder how far your own great worldliness has carried you, through time and change and space.

From you such words as *perverse* or *immoral* never emerged, it's true. *Seduction* did trouble you, but you made no distinction between varieties. *My dearest child, come go with me, such glorious games I will play with you.* After all, you scorned Mr. Davenport for the way he got Lucy and Nellie and Karla melting for him. No one melted for you, Anna. You made no cunning analyses to charm us, no seduction — well, not of that sort anyway.

There was no tinge of eroticism between four earnest, eventually homosexual, teenagers and a stern old lady from the days of the Kaiser.

But a kind of seduction nonetheless? The word means "a leading apart or astray"— not all that different, really, from *education*, with its promise of liberation, of rescue from the dark —"a leading out from." But *apart* and *astray* presuppose, somewhere, a straight path, and you of all people never believed in such a thing. No, you urged us apart. Or shall we say you knew, you'd already seen, how alone we were in the Upholstery City, how far we had already strayed from others? Is that why you chose us and took us in?

But what essence had you seen through to? How far inside? What voices within us had you heard? Was it simply your Old World upbringing that respected our privacy? Or did you divine the thing in us that Americans called queer but you interpreted as merely foreign to the ways of Quissick and therefore, to you, appealingly familiar? But how familiar would we seem now in the wholeness of our middle age, in our living stories filled with hope and dismay? Oh Anna, we're glad you're dead and won't be brought back to us now, eighty-seven years old, in a state of high temper. Back then you didn't have to know yet.

And Malcolm and Henry didn't either. Secrecy had intruded once again. Rupert and Kip, somewhat confused by their new obsession, didn't dare speak of it to their two closest friends. They didn't even speak of it themselves, hoping, fearing it was some passing stage, a trial run for something even more wonderful still to come with girls they hadn't imagined knowing yet. At times Kip or Rupert would find himself wishing the foursome would somehow keep the two of them from being alone together again. But there are days in a week, weeks in a season, time keeps at it, and enticing moments come around again, half unwished for as they may be.

RUPERT'S Aunt Undine had finally shut down the belching furnace and settled into a summer mood, curtains drawn all the tighter against the sun, grimy rotating fans on floor and shelf, six or seven of them, whirring at all hours, wafting dust balls about her rooms. But up the stairs, with shadeless windows wide in Quissick's June stillness, the four of us would still gather. Eleventh grade was over, and you, Anna, had retreated to the summer house of an old friend by a lake in New Hampshire, so we were free of you. We could read and talk and argue and not fear your judgment. Neither could we receive your guidance. Something summery went lax in us.

Kip discovered the novels of Nabokov and began to agonize over his split literary loyalties — sloppily beat or supremely elegant. His easygoing parents never expected him to work, except about the house. Henry had to put in his full shift at the lumberyard. Malcolm took a job not, for once, at the Phipps pharmacy but as office boy for *The Quissick Quotidian*. And Rupert, early every morning, pedaled the old bike Kip had salvaged for him from the Skerritt garage south to the hog farms (as they're no longer called) to work at that vegetable stand, the giant concrete pumpkin on the Southbridge Road — remember it, Anna?

But a certain spring night still hung over us all, whether we knew it or not. Tired of an argument the other two were having about whether Rupert tried too hard to be anarchic or just genuinely was so, Malcolm and Henry had gone meandering to savor the lilacky air, all the way down to the Worcester Road in Upper Quiddy, across the vast vacant lot that is now the Quidnapunxet Mall, up past their old middle school where they retold seventh-grade dirty jokes ("You think that's disgusting? You should see how we make our doughnuts"— never mind, Anna) and felt nostalgic and silly, then on under moonlit Parapet Ridge, sensing the delicious pressure in their bursting brains — so much still to say, to see, to do. On their corner for parting, reluctant to head up home yet, Henry confessed an odd thing about his recent performance: that in order to feel he had become the character, the drummer boy in the opera, he had tried thinking of himself as Rupert. "I just couldn't think of myself as Henry Vigneault up there," he tried to explain to Malcolm. "I had to become someone else, someone crazier, someone not at all me. So I decided I'd pretend I was Rupert, as if it was Rupert Eid onstage not me, and that somehow did it. I didn't put that in my essay because it would sound sort of sicko, wouldn't it?" "I know what you mean though," said Malcolm hesitantly. Then Henry: "Maybe it's part of performing, but it felt a little perverted." "Well, I wouldn't tell Rupert," said Malcolm, who didn't want to remember right then how he too used to imagine himself being, if not Rupert, then at least like Rupert back when he had first met him and found him so intriguing. Without even the excuse of playing a role, he had almost wanted to become a sort of Rupert in his dusty empty upper floors, odd as that still seemed to him. He had actually felt himself somehow losing his lifelong Phippsness, and now it made him feel suddenly hollow to think of it. He and Henry said their good nights quietly, a bit distracted, each in his own curious thoughts.

And was Undine Eid snoring soundly in her four-poster, or was she on the prowl, peeking out her curtains at the moon? Had she heard only two boys leave, counted the number of footfalls on the stairs?

Her Rupert was becoming lost to her. He still brought the groceries home, he took out the trash. Occasionally, he sat with her and read a book, ex libris HUTCHINS, from the glass-fronted bookcases, but if she spoke, interrupting, he'd leave her room. Only when he was eating could she get him to listen to her, so she'd hobble into the kitchen, collapse on a chair, and begin: "Michael Tavistock is late with the check this month. After all my years in that family. I wrote him. The letter is by the door. You will mail it? My brother, you know, used to send me little pins for those Tavistock boys: 'Macht durch Freude,' you know, from his youth camp. Mister and Missus would not like it, so I always kept them our secret. Those boys had a collection. David was like my own Hitler-Jüngling. I had him march with me carrying the little paper flag your father sent over, up and down in the laundry yard. She caught us at it. Jesus Maria! But what did I know about another war coming? I missed my brother only. He was younger than you when I saw him the last time. I had to play instead with those babies of the Tavistocks. Esther, she was my enemy. She would not have me comb her. I was lonesome for you, well, I mean for Sintram. You look the same, Rupert. If I have saved the little paper flag I will make you hold it for me to pretend you are my brother, okay?" "You always ask me that, Aunt. You don't have that flag anymore, but I wouldn't hold it if you did, I'd tear it up and spit on it." "Rupert, why do you speak to me so?" "Aunt, one day you're jabbering about Nazis being to blame for everything, for you losing your brother, and then another day you're dreaming of happy Hitler-Jünglings." "And Mrs. Tavistock always promised she would take care of us forever. After the war, then she would bring my brother over to me, he would work here too, and when he had a nice bride, that was good. Oh, Missus was going to do everything for me. And that gottverdammter Hitler, so stupid! I would kill that man if I could see him." "Good for you, Aunt," said half-listening Rupert who had heard every word a hundred times before. He rinsed off his plate, capped the can of tuna with wax paper and a rubber band, tucked it in the fridge and escaped.

If she nabbed him again in the front hall on his way out for the evening, grabbing his elbow to hold him a minute, she'd ask him about those other boys, his friends. "Do not go to their houses, Rupert. Their families are not good people. I know the Tavistocks, how they were. They are all like that here in Quissick. They are such liars here, Rupert. They only want to make you a slave, they have no place for you." "I'm taking some money from the jar,

Aunt. Maybe I'll go to a movie at the Valley." "And my letter to Michael Tavistock."

She became used to Kip showing up without the others. He treated her politely, even if she did look at him with suspicion, and in time she softened toward him; in the summer, without his leather jacket and boots, he may have seemed less dangerous. "So you are now Rupert's buddy?" "Well, I've been his buddy for a year," Kip replied, picking up on her carefully American term. "Maybe now you can make him stop reading all the time. It is not good for his eyes." "But he loves reading, Miss Eid." "No, but it is not so good if he does it always. Michael and David Tavistock did not read so many books. You do not make money in this country if you read books too much. All his life he will be working in a pumpkin."

On hot afternoons, when Henry got off work, he'd arrive in a Vigneault Lumber truck in front of the Quotidian Building, at Common and Ninth, and coax Malcolm into taking an early supper break, then they'd swoop up Opossum Hill and Kip would roll out of the hammock, *Lolita* in hand, and the three would drive along Railroad Avenue till it turned into the Southbridge Road, out to the vegetable stand, orange and squat by the roadside. Rupert would lift his bike over the tailgate, and Kip, shirtless, would join him in the back, stretching out not to waste any sun. The four of us were off to the Quisquabaug Ponds.

Sometimes we stopped at the beach on Bottom Pond to say hi to Io, but our usual route was to hop the stream and walk up the west shore of Top Pond to a shady grassy spot where Kip relinquished the sun in favor of the company. He had spent a rather lonesome day mowing the lawn or

painting the garage, throwing sticks for the family retriever or baby-sitting Oops for a couple of hours. Cato
went to a sports camp to keep him out of trouble; Io was at
the beach all day giggling with her girlfriends; Kip had suc-
cessfully banished Connel and Coral, when they returned
from their play group, from within fifty feet of his hammock, unless summoned — Stay cool, cats, man, you bug
me, he told them and that did it.

Malcolm never looked quite comfortable by the pond.
There'd be ants or mosquitoes, or too many stones under
the grass. He'd pull off his jeans and look especially awkward in his baggy boxers. The middle of his chest sort of
sank in, and when he edged himself over the pebbles into
the water he acted like a grandpa. Henry was the exuber-
ant one, Anna, as you can imagine. He dived and splashed
and headed out across the pond under water, which always
unnerved Rupert, who never went in no matter how hot it
got. Kip was a floater. He'd paddle around in his QHS
shorts, brown and relaxed. Henry would surface, dripping,
the racing suit he wore bunched up around his buttocks.
We watched each other closely back then; all high school
boys do, of course, aware of how differently their bodies
are changing, afraid of what the differences will mean in
life. Rupert would go only as far as to unbutton his shirt,
exposing a pale flatness, and roll up his pant legs above his
slim calves.

"Do you think I'm cooled off enough?" Malcolm would
ask after two minutes in Quisquabaug. "Shouldn't I get
back to the office?" But he'd have to lie on the lumpy grass
to dry off his shorts, and he and Rupert might talk a bit in
their old private way, as in their early friendship. "You're

sort of hard to get to, Eid, I feel cut off from you lately," said Malcolm once. "Why do you say that?" said Rupert, stretching as if he was bored. "Well, we don't have any of our good talks anymore." "Yes we do." "But I mean about the private things, like our childhoods, or about Uncle Abraham or your aunt. We always used to confide in each other." "We've been over all that, Phipps. What's still to say?" "But it feels like something's missing from you lately," said Malcolm.

Anna, we won't drag you along through every emotional imbalance a set of four people has endured, but you can imagine us that summer, Kip floating about in secretive sensual bliss, Henry diving and reappearing breathlessly, Rupert and Malcolm in serious deadlock. It had probably always been inside Malcolm, but even as he worked so enthusiastically for the newspaper, an aspect of him was emerging that assumed rejection — a sad Malcolm, an ignored Malcolm.

Now here we sit on this Caribbean veranda belonging to Professor Howard, the islander gone north. Malcolm is with us still of course, and we're bouncing our words back and forth in the soft heat, elaborating, pondering, emending, surprising each other. Only because we know our subject so well, only because you once set us talking together, thinking together — and maybe it's also the beer in the afternoon, the rum after dinner, and these breezes and the pounding of those waves, beats of time, one after another like collisions of huge trucks, Anna, or like an immense foundry hammering out behemoths. At night, the walls of the bungalow seem ready to fall in, shatter, even though we're high above the battered sands.

In the mornings it's Henry who rushes down, timing it carefully between breakers, to swim out and ride the splendid crests. Once or twice Rupert has dared to join him. This sea is different, he says, from the cool flat ponds. He's overcome his water fear now; he's drawn to it. Henry takes his hand and pulls him out, quick, beyond danger, and once there Rupert rides entranced; he's never felt anything like it, he says. Kip and Malcolm are more cautious. There's a little backwater where a ghaut (they call it) empties warm volcanic springs into the sea, and there Kip can float and Malcolm peacefully wade. We have our ten-day retreat, Anna, this resounding bay tucked between cliffs. Not the hushed afternoons beside Top Pond, but we are the same four, your four, and we've loved each other all these years. See what you've given us? And like that summer, without you, we are once more in limbo.

What was it like beside your New Hampshire lake? You didn't know us for three whole months, we didn't know you: an intimation of the permanent loss we'd suffer in less than a year. Students don't think of their teachers as having other lives. It was enough of a jolt for us to come upon you in your Plymouth turning that corner in Plashing Falls, or for Rupert to catch a glimpse of your shape at Christmastime in your frosty window. We'd imagined you lived only in your art, which was Instruction. To think of you with a husband, or husbands, with daughters left behind in Europe, even with friends — one single friend. No, summer was for us an expansive time, but when it was over we expected you to reappear unchanged. We'd consigned you to some miraculous estivation.

But a letter came to the *Quotidian*, the only address

where you could reach us and avoid adult scrutiny. Malcolm, suddenly remembering it while pulling on his pants at the pond, withdrew an envelope, slightly creased, from his back pocket. *Dear ones,* you wrote in tight squiggles, *I am peaceful here.* Strange to read your written English, without accent, not quite yours. *My friend, Mrs. Bump* (it looked like, but it couldn't have been, could it?) *has let me inhabit a tiny cottage, away from her grandchildren and their tennis, and I do a lot of reading, take a long swim, and my old friend, who comes here all the way from Chicago, visits me on my screened porch and we talk to remind us of Spain and our glorious days. She is the first American I ever knew well. She introduced me to my American husband when once I found myself in this country. You shall have an old friend like her someday. It is life's reward. What do you read? Kip is certainly among the avant-garde. Do they let you write for their paper, Malcolm? What do you sing, Henry? And how is my Rupert amid the alien corn? You see, I think of all of you even as I retrace my own past. Mrs. Bump* (there it was again, but we couldn't be sure of it) *tells me I speak too much about my boys. With friendly wishes for your happy summer, Anna Aylmer.* There was no address for us to write you back, only a smeared postmark.

"I wonder if Aylmer's a lesbian," said Malcolm. "But why? Just because she goes to see her old friend?" asked Kip. "She's been married two or three times, and this Mrs. Bump or whoever's got grandchildren." "That doesn't necessarily mean anything," said the wiser Malcolm. See how we high school boys puzzled over you, Anna? What was Malcolm imagining — two naked ladies in their sixties, splashing about in the moonlight and mosquitoes, two Spanish Civil War loyalists, ardent in their reunion?

It's odd, Anna — we've been meaning to tell you what's become of us, but like you and Mrs. Bump we can't help retracing ourselves. Could we ever have known then how we might fit into the world now? You, of all people, who lived so many disconnected lives, you should understand that we cannot have stayed the same four fellows you once thought you'd fathomed. We have gone on remaking those essential selves you claimed to have discovered in each of us, and all the memorabilia we may have assembled cannot, yet, fix us to a page in Malcolm's album any more than we can fix you there. Be patient, Anna, we'll come eventually to our current incarnations. But through our seventeen-year-old eyes we find ourselves rediscovering you, and the sight of you was always encouraging to us. You were the first adult to treat us as your peers.

L OST AS *the past may seem, render it clearly*... Your admonishment, Anna, the poem you wrote for us at graduation — its central image, the candle flame, suggests you meant "render" in the sense of "melt" or "boil down." So here we sit, rendering you for ourselves. Do you mind? We can each still recite your poem, not missing a word. After your death it echoed secretly as your epitaph in each of our perplexed souls: *Now you are leaving me, go without minding*... But a week earlier those lines had evoked merely the end of our high school days. How could we then have ever imagined we had really left you?

It was in senior year that we came at last to know you better. The letter from the lake really began it. *She introduced me to my American husband* — what a thrill to read that sentence the first time! Were we actually going to discover more secrets of Anna Aylmer? Had she singled us out for confidences entrusted to no one else in Quissick? What had anyone else ever known of you beyond the details Malcolm's Uncle Abraham had somehow scraped up in his snooping, years ago?

"She's an odd duck." That's what he'd told Malcolm when he heard you'd chosen us. "Surfaced mysteriously at the high school toward the end of the war, when you were a gurgling baby. Mrs. Aylmer, but without a Mister. I was always on the lookout for lonesome ladies. Approaching forty myself then, and she wasn't all that much older. No beauty, oh no, but ladies of a certain age, Malcolm, are repositories of flaming passions. Remember that when your time comes. I met this Aylmer woman at a school tea. The powers that be were still tolerating me at that point. The war, Mal — they needed what few defective males they could muster on the home front. She took my hand, but what a chilly stare she had! Stopped me cold. I must say, Mal, you're maturing rapidly, my boy. Any day now you'll find yourself in the boudoir of an eager divorcée twice your age and you must tell me all about her." Malcolm had been instructed not to let Uncle Abraham turn his talk in a suggestive direction. "It's only talk, of course," his mother assured him, "but it's a mistake to let him go on, he works himself up so. Whenever he starts on one of those subjects, you know, Malcolm, just get him talking about his stamp collection." That's what Malcolm had to cope with at home, Anna.

But he couldn't help trying to find out more about you from that gawking, piercing-eyed uncle. "A man of enforced leisure discovers a great deal, Mal. That Aylmer woman perturbed me. I decided to investigate. Not that she would give me the merest smile, oh no, but I contrived to bump into her at the library or when she stopped for morning coffee at Boyle's. Once, only once, I managed to produce a response. 'And how have you found it here in

Quissick, Mrs. Aylmer?' I asked her, and she said something about it being a pleasant refuge. Must have caught her at an especially lonesome hour. 'After three wars and three husbands,' says she into her coffee cup, 'anyone might be seeking refuge, not so?' Kraut accent. But that's all she would say. You may well imagine, with this talk of three husbands, I found myself all the more intrigued. But shortly, Boyle appeared and asked me either to leave the lady alone or get out."

Everything else Uncle Abraham told Malcolm may have been fabricated. He portrayed you as a secret agent, Anna; he'd seen you poring over "clandestine documents" at the Quissick library, translating them no doubt into Russian. He claimed to have delved through the files before he was barred from QHS and to have found you had come to us by way of Chicago — Mrs. Bump's Chicago — warmly recommended by a Marxist pedagogue at the university, who had some curious connection, it seemed, with our very own Tavistocks. Strange bedfellows the war made of Communist and Patriot! Then once, he'd overheard you speaking into the phone, long distance apparently. " 'Since the fighting began I have hardly been able to live with myself for abandoning her there'" was the line Uncle Abraham reported to Malcolm, filtered through years of his fanciful embellishments. Still, we stored those words away, part of the legend of our Señora, along with that curious pronouncement you'd made the week before our García Lorca misunderstanding: *You see, muchachos, dejé mi alma en España. What is alma, Señor Skerritt? Your brother Cato would know. Yes — Soul! I left my Soul in Spain. Mi Alma que peleaba junto a mi ha quedado en España. My Alma that fought beside me. You catch?* Kip scribbled in approximate Spanish those enigmatic lines in his notebook to see what Cato could make of them, doubtful as he was of his brother's expertise. We were as fanciful as Abraham Phipps in our innocent way. We imagined you were speaking to us, in code, of a daughter. Later, we pieced it together with what you'd said about the Kaiser's Berlin. We worked it out: an imaginary Prussian soldier-student, imaginarily killed at the front, had left you with an imaginary child, her imaginary name was Alma, and she was to follow you, twenty years later, to fight in the Spanish Civil War.

*"Vor Madrid im Schützengraben, in der Stunde der Gefahr,"* you sang shakily along with those scratchy records of loyalist songs. In the trenches outside Madrid, in the hour of danger . . . Against all the Spanish, Italian and German fascists on the one side, there stood beside their Spanish brothers Italians, Germans, French, English, Americans, leftists and communists and democrats, the United Front, the International Brigade, the Thälmann-Bataillon. *"Spaniens Himmel breitet seine Sterne über uns're Schützengräben aus,"* you sang to us, and Henry joined in phonetically (he sings German beautifully now) — Spain's heaven spreads its stars out over our trenches . . . We scarcely dared speak afterwards because the melody seemed to have gone so deeply into you.

That summer we had all these pieces of you to meditate on. Your letter, in your absence, became a talisman, each of us in possession of it for a number of days before passing it on. Our eyes saw a tiny cottage by a lake, and we heard, in the far distance, the comforting whop of tennis balls, the Bump grandchildren's high-pitched squeals and, closer up, ripples lapping at rocks and, in a rocking chair, an old lady — older than you, we decided, this Mrs. Bump, because even you needed a mentor, Anna. The lesbian possibility persisted vaguely. Had Aylmer himself been only a means to grant you permanent asylum? Was it a very narrow escape you had from the Old World? *The homeland is far* . . .

But it wasn't so much your legendary past as that lazy idyllic present that haunted us. When Kip and Rupert curled up asleep on any number of wide mahogany beds, they heard your night lake sounds. When Henry, sleepless, gazed out from the Ridge over Quissick, he hummed your songs. "Die Heimat ist weit . . ." And from Uncle Abraham's knocks on his locked bedroom door, Malcolm protected himself with the idea that you would be coming back to us and leading us out of this tight small world we had always inhabited.

OUT OF — and apart. We wanted it so much, Anna, fearful as we were, and you helped us confirm the direction we'd already taken. Rupert, of course, had always been singular; Kip, in his large family, had been fighting to isolate himself for years; now Henry had his yearnings as well, and they were fortified by you. Malcolm's case was less clear, but all the more urgent. Your characterization (you insisted on characterizing us): *Malcolm is the one who shall always be the most polite and untroubling to his tribe. He is the blessed boy. His mother would not need to say "Am I not the lucky mother?" In his family it is not spoken. He knows how good he must be. It would be extra to make a point of it. The mother of Kip may complain of those awful black boots, but the mother of Malcolm never of his handsome pullover. It is by approval that such a tribe possesses its offspring, nicht?*

That hot summer Kip showed up once on Malcolm's day off, rang the much painted over bell so familiar from his grammar school best friendship, and Mrs. Phipps opened the door with a start. "Kip Skerritt, when did we last see your smiling face? Malcolm's just out with Pop for a driving lesson. It's lovely to see you, sweetie," and she kissed him on his cheek, a firm kiss, as if he were still a boy.

They sat in the living room, a bit awkwardly, Kip remembers, a sense of tense quiet behind each closed door — where was old Uncle Abraham lurking? The Phipps house had impressed itself on Kip's soul, a trim tidy antidote to his own (which flew apart at the joints). The furniture here was from an earlier unupholstered Quissick, a Quissick not of factories and warehouses but of workshops, of craftsmen. No heavy Victorian mahogany handed down to the nurserymaid, no overstuffed prewar catalog standbys collapsing under an assault of Skerritts nor the plush modern comforts of the Maison Vigneault — Phipps furniture was brittle, tippy, not to be leaned against, treasurable if it ever were to find itself in a Boston antique store, but destined to be passed on matter-of-factly to daughter Louisa and son Malcolm and their descendants and theirs. In fifth grade, suddenly aware of such distinctions, Kip had badgered his mother to purge their own house of clutter and get some plain straight-backed chairs, but she'd simply whooped at him, so Kip had to visit this house on Fourteenth Street if he wanted refinement. Malcolm is still Kip's final arbiter; Kip never quite trusts himself until Malcolm gives the nod. In his little house in Lower Quiddy near Quissick State, where he teaches, Professor Clifford Skerritt strives for a Phippsian spareness but finds himself accumulating his own version of clutter despite all efforts at chucking out — to Rupert's constant amusement.

"Tell me about yourself," said Mrs. Phipps fondly. "Oh, Malcolm keeps me posted, but you boys are always out on the town now. Those lovely days of coming over to play, which as far as I could tell with you boys meant to talk — I know you had your lotto games, Malcolm's model cars, stamps, whatever, but I never heard small boys talk so much when I'd have expected vroom-vroom!" "We still mostly talk," Kip said, relaxing (almost) on the bench by the fireplace, hard cool wood against his bare thighs. "Louisa considers you and Malcolm partners in crime. 'Why isn't Kip Skerritt working at the paper too?' she said to me just last night." Then Mrs. Phipps, jaggedly bony where Malcolm was merely angular (he looks more like her now), fixed Kip with her eyes: "Louisa's awful envious of that special class of yours with Frau Aylmer. She always admired that woman. Louisa says she'd have been better prepared for college if she'd had someone rigorous like that taking an interest in her." "It's rough going sometimes though," said Kip. "Of course, Louisa's done fine on her own," Mrs. Phipps was careful to point out. "Pharmacology isn't as plain a matter as it once was. Already she's got Pop beat on his own turf."

Louisa Phipps still lives at home, Anna. Uncle Abraham is gone (after some terrible years), Mr. Phipps is incapacitated, Mrs. Phipps frail, and now Louisa runs the drugstore. She's wonderful with Malcolm's daughters when they come east to be with him for the summer and he brings them out to Quissick. She keeps a correspondence going with them all year.

When Malcolm got back from that driving lesson, surprised as he was to find his mother chatting with Kip, he announced he had to pedal right over to the office to check up on something or other mumble mumble. But his mother wouldn't let him go without a full report on the driving, and when Mr. Phipps came in she had to hear it all from his point of view too. "And the parallel parking this time?" As always, Malcolm perked right up under maternal cross-questioning. You were right, Anna: in some ways Malcolm needed you more than any of us.

He wouldn't bike over alongside Kip up Opossum Hill but took the fast route on Fourteenth to Common, pedaling furiously — and worrying: "I'm sure I forgot to put that police report in Oglesby's box. Please don't let him be there yet. And I've had it with Skerritt. He's only dropping by because he figures he ought to, once in a while still, on his own. But what else does he have to do anyway? And I've had it with Eid too. They're both such drifters. What are they ever going to accomplish in this world?"

This annoyance, though it persisted, couldn't quite declare itself in public. Malcolm still went to the ponds, still joined the others on Rupert's roof and, most of the time, seemed perfectly happy.

Henry was entirely unaware of Malcolm's jealous undercurrent. He was working for his father, and when he wasn't working he was swimming, and when he wasn't swimming he was singing. He'd found the thing that made sense of life, and out of his certainty, by the end of summer, his voice was developing a deep velvetiness. Soteropoulos was eyeing him for the Arcadian shepherd in next year's QLO production. His new voice teacher, Barry Rosenwald at Quissick State, had him trying Schubert and Mahler lieder and mélodies of Fauré and Ravel. Henry even worked at his piano playing, the better to accompany his practicing. All his romantic longings must have been subsumed in that music. When he sang of Fauré's Lydia or Ravel's Dulcinée, of Schubert's Müllerin or Mahler's *zwei blauen Augen*, the rest of us imagined a Henry devoted to no Nellie or Karla or Lucy of our own set but to some lithe girl (as it would have to be) whom he might have once seen at Bottom Pond, someone's visiting cousin probably never to be glimpsed again. Henry, our yearner, maybe he felt it first: something was going to shake us in the coming year, something to make new people of us. One heat-heavy silent afternoon, he burst dripping out of Quisquabaug's depths, spluttering, "But am I crazy, children?! I want this summer to be already over!"

His underwater swimming was evidence of his lung capacity. To sustain a note, to let it swell then fade with no hint of breathlessness, is a requirement of his art. Your Henry, Anna, has sung with real orchestras, in real opera productions; he's given recitals in real concert halls, been praised in real newspapers beyond the close ring of the somehow not-quite-so-real Quidnapunxet Valley. Does it come as a surprise, Anna, that he's actually made a real recording? Imagine Reger's "Requiem," our very own poem — Soul, forget them not — with full chorus and orchestra at a music festival in New Hampshire, your Henry's solo preserved pristine. And records don't even get scratchy anymore. Nothing will ever make them sound old like those crackly seventy-eights of yours from the Spanish Civil War. There aren't any grooves to wear out: the music is encoded in millions of tiny pits and read by a thread of light. Don't ask us how, we barely understood grooves.

Though Henry isn't exactly a star, he's steadily booked — always off to Utica or Fargo or some such town to become the Dutchman or Figaro or the Toreador. It took him two years to save enough from the lumberyard so he could go to Boston. When his father came to believe Henry really meant it, he sent him to study further in Düsseldorf; Henry was the first of us, Anna, to make it back to your world. Amidst all the Americans who populate German opera houses, he eventually got some small parts. And with Kip plodding away at a thesis, with Malcolm bouncing from San Francisco suburban paper to Boston suburban paper, three of us at least were establishing ourselves. When Henry finally came back home with enough credits to aspire to the American opera circuit, we found ourselves, all four, for a brief span in the same city once again. Of course, Boston is much larger than Quissick, but as we approached thirty, in our separate ways, we felt at home there. That was 1972, ten years after you'd gone for the last time chugging up the Parapet in your Plymouth. Perhaps you'd have had a hard time recognizing us, Anna, harder than you would now that the selves you once fathomed have fully emerged from our faces and we no longer try to overlay them with one mask or another. We were at our farthest from what you saw in us, and so your old characterizations seemed all wrong: were we free of you, at last?

The three already settled Bostonians had planned to welcome the wanderer home. Malcolm, recently divorced, and Kip, who had the only car among us (a silver-blue Valiant with one gold replacement door panel), were to pick up Rupert on the way to the airport. Malcolm winced out the passenger window as the neighborhoods grew shabbier. "Maybe this reminds him of Plashing Falls in the old days," he said. "But he's doing better, Malcolm, really he is," said Kip, "you just didn't know how bad he got when you were still out in California." "But you told me he's still not really eating," said Malcolm. Kip let his face go slack with sudden hopelessness. "You're still seeing him though?" Malcolm asked, "I mean, by seeing him, well . . ." "Occasionally," said Kip, "when he'll let me." Malcolm was watching the numbers along a treeless avenue. He hadn't yet visited Rupert in this rooming house of his. Since returning from the West, Malcolm had only bumped into him at a bar or a party, but he knew the street number well — he'd often written Rupert during the divorce year. When Kip pulled the car over and swung open the golden door, Malcolm felt suddenly squeamish. "Shall I wait down here?" he asked.

Anna, it is awkward to reintroduce ourselves at this stage. We like ourselves in high school better than these late-twenties sorts. Were you at all like us at a corresponding point? We've read about Berlin after the First War, but what were you up to there? Did you ever go dancing beside male couples at some decadent club? We can only guess at what may have been your expressionist period.

Malcolm, carefully locking his door, followed Kip up the brownstone steps. No glass in these doors, only plywood panels with scribbles about niggers and faggots. Kip's shiny black hair was so long, Anna, he'd hold it off his face with a red bandanna or tie it into a tail in back or sometimes both at once. This wasn't considered particularly flamboyant, you must understand: the chairman of one of his English departments wore his hair similarly. In blue jeans and blue work shirt and that same style of black engineer boot with thick heel and jingling buckle, Kip appeared before classrooms of freshmen at three different colleges, trying to keep up with his rent and — here it comes, Anna — his psychiatrist bills. *But, Kinder, you do not simply go to a psychiatrist. What was it, my dearest one, tell me. What was wrong?* See how we imagine, forever, the deep well of your concern for us? And at the same time, your suspicion of our American ways with matters of the soul.

But it was actually Malcolm, ever the anti-Freudian, whom you would have been most worried about. He wasn't so long haired as to require a bandanna, but his tidiness had relaxed into the baggy comfort of a frayed tweed jacket, a loosened tie, and a pair of jeans instead of the corduroys he has now long since reverted to. But he'd had to leave his two daughters behind him in California, and he felt it, every hour of the day. Two daughters, Louisa and Anna — yes: Anna. But he left them behind with Martha, his fellow poli sci grad student ex-wife — Martha Hooper she was again, no longer Martha Hooper Phipps. She'd wiped Malcolm out of her life and had custody eleven months of the year, but Anna and Louisa still spend every July with their father in Massachusetts.

Kip had knocked, then hammered on the plywood panel, had finally bellowed into the hole in the doorframe where a bell had once lodged. "It wouldn't surprise me," he told Malcolm, "if he's gone out, or completely forgotten. Or if he's taking the subway and will claim that's what I told him to do." "The door's open," said Malcolm twisting the knob.

They climbed three flights to 44, which was open and

empty of Rupert. The smoke-stained window rattled in the April wind. This place was not merely dusty, like his Aunt Undine's house, but grimy, caked, smelling of decades of cigarettes and cats. Two blankets, red and black, were bunched up on a mattress, and along the walls were toppling piles of molding old books. Rupert collected things only to sell them; he had purged himself of all he had ever owned. "What's he reading?" Malcolm asked, pointing to a tome nestled in the blankets. Kip shrugged, so Malcolm knelt down to see: *Anna Karenina.* "Come on, let's get out of here," said Kip. But here came Rupert up the stairs from the bathroom on the floor below. "Oh." "Didn't you hear me shouting?" "Uh-uh." "Ru, we'll be late." "Welcome, Malcolm," said Rupert, who looked almost as coated in grime as the walls of his room, his hair as tangled as the blankets, eyes clouded as the windowpane. "What's Henry going to make of you, Eid?" said Malcolm, and Rupert countered, "He wrote me from Germany how maybe we could get a place together." Kip, at the door, turned around. "Henry and you?" "Why not?" said Rupert. "You and I'd be terrible living together, Kip, but I could live with Henry, easy."

It was going to take some balancing, the four of us being together again. Kip, in the minute it took to descend to the car, was deciding that he and Rupert were finally absolutely finished. Not that they'd always been faithful to each other. *Well, I am no puritan, dear ones. It is you Americans who are puritans.* But, Anna, you might have discovered your puritan streak had you lived to those years. It had gone far beyond the life you finally allowed us a glimpse of, well into twelfth grade, when you had us reading *Madame Bovary* and asked us not to let it be known. *There are those who might object, children,* you said conspiratorially, leaning across your desk, arms spread as if to encompass us in a marvelous inner circle. *I have some experience with American attitudes,* you said. And then you whispered, confirming the rumor officially: *You see, I myself have had three actual husbands. This is not a pleasing piece of information in Quissick. And before them — well, you are old enough now — my first child out of wedlock, dear ones. My own dear little soul, born there in Berlin just before the Armistice, but fatherless, you see. And four years till I found Herr Ulrich, the father of my second. Then I became the respectable Anna Ulrich. Oh if my own family had been of some prominence, then perhaps I would have become Anna Ulrich Klumpp — not Klumpp Ulrich as you Americans put it. But Klumpp you see is a not very pretty name. I was glad to leave it, ja! You are men. You will never have to change your names.*

We lived, senior year, for those rare minutes in class when something set you off the track, when our eager eyes would nudge you further in legendary revelation. We never dared ask questions, we only watched you, hopefully. But something, finally, would tip you back to the proper topic. *Puritans! Oh yes, you see, it is only an American who would write a* Moby-Dick. *It is a book without women, n'est-ce pas! Americans are not ever quite romantics. They must be visionaries, isn't it! Beware, my dear ones. It is left for me to teach you about women, to teach real life. And so, page one. "Nous étions à l'étude." We were at our studies . . .*

Here on this island, Kip has brought along his class notebooks, Malcolm his old albums, the better to call you up out of our past. We can always hear your answers because we'll hear forever the rhythms of your speech singing in our brains; still, an occasional exact quote, feverishly jotted down, a translated poem, a foreign phrase — these are the snippets we can conjure with.

We have no such notebooks from our years together in Boston and no single voice like yours drawing us together. To set beside our memories we have only Malcolm's newspaper articles, Kip's abandoned dissertations, Henry's concert programs — all addressed outward, to the world not to each other. We were looking beyond, preparing for our larger lives to come, and not the least nostalgic. Nostalgia lay in the fibers of high school, but over the first years of work life, does one imagine reminiscing? *Lost as the past may seem* . . . We'd as soon have left it back there, good and lost.

So now, for you, some portraits from our rootless time.

We set out in the Valiant through the twisty short streets of Boston's underbelly, Kip turning suddenly to avoid an apparent jam two blocks ahead or cursing the lane he found himself consigned to. Malcolm had been expecting to ride in back, but Rupert had quickly squeezed in there before he could make the offer. Malcolm was just as glad, because he worried about proper back support, but he also knew that every small move of Rupert's was, in Kip's eyes, a sort of sign. Had Rupert taken the front seat, Kip would now be driving more relaxedly. "What's the hurry," he'd be saying, "enjoy the magnolias, the spring sunlight on the bricks." But Rupert had sat glumly behind, and Kip was now fuming at the prospect of his living with Henry, further out of reach once more.

Malcolm wasn't sure what it meant for an adult still to be in love with his high school pal. When Kip had cross-questioned him, Malcolm admitted he hadn't quite known what it meant to be in love with Martha Hooper either. What had started as a happy meeting of minds had never quite been a happy meeting of bodies. Was it the same for Kip and Rupert? Actually, it seemed the opposite now. Rupert could always revive Kip with a touch, and he knew how long he could stave him off too. And Kip traipsed weekly to his psychiatrist to figure out why he couldn't get over Rupert, couldn't give up on him in a dozen years of never quite being together. Was this in the very nature of the homosexual attraction itself, Malcolm wondered, or in Kip's low estimation of himself? The odd truth was that Rupert exercised an equivalent power — though not a sexual one — over Malcolm. Rupert was the person he would always drop everything to go see, to cheer up, to help, and Rupert never had to ask for assistance or attention. He lay on his mattress, shivering and sniffly and underfed, and read and read — and that was enough.

When we emerged from the tunnel and swung around into the parking lot for international arrivals, we realized the significance of what was about to occur. Rupert, after his long silence in the car, expressed it first. "It feels like we're all going to meet our long lost brother." "I was thinking the same," said Kip, warmed by Rupert's "our," by evidence of such feeling. "I was thinking," Kip said, picking up his stride toward the terminal, "that we're our own family in a way, the four of us, and we'll always be.

Henry's been away and none of us has felt quite right. When Malcolm was away too, maybe for a time it seemed like that was it, the end of something. But we've circled back now, one by one. We're all about to be here again."

That was what Malcolm felt too, even more so, perhaps, after his own transplantations to California and back, but he didn't say anything as he followed Kip and Rupert, now side by side, into the echoing hall where relatives and friends hovered outside two black automatic doors watching strangers issue forth every minute or two. Kip took up a position deep in the crowd, and there, by the doors, he saw the anxious faces of Blanche Germaine and Guy Vigneault, Henry's younger sister and brother. Of course, Maman would have sent them. And was Henry to be whisked right off to Quissick? Our three hearts quickened in our chests.

BUT EVENTUALLY, Anna, Henry returned to Boston. Our first evening, just us four, with Blanche and Guy tucked back in the valley to the west where none of us imagined ever settling down again, took place at Malcolm's small apartment in the Back Bay.

We sat around the cherrywood table, a Phipps heirloom out of their attic, water stained and chipped with the kind of family wear that endows a simple piece of furniture with visible history. The creaky uncomfortable chairs, at four different stages of collapse, carried us back to a Quissick evening more than ten years past when on those same chairs we'd sat about Malcolm's mother's kitchen consuming three large pizzas and a dozen Cokes. We didn't often invade the Phippses, but we'd been to a football game at school, an event we took interest in only because, at last, Quissick was up against Leominster for an elusive championship and even you were going, Anna, doing your bit for school spirit. *Monsieur Simone insisted, dear ones. The language teachers must wave the flag. It was all so very muddy, wasn't it?*

And there, in Malcolm's Back Bay apartment, with no room to navigate between daybed, cluttered desktop and chair legs, we talked again about what we'd talked about then, about you, Anna, perched on the bleachers beside our dangerously rotund French teacher murmuring your bafflement into his ear as the crowd roared. "When she shook the pom-pom Lucy Idlenot handed up to her, she looked like she wasn't sure if she was doing it right . . ." "And Monsieur wanted one, too . . ." We may have been repeating the very same words we'd said back then, high on so much sugar and a riotous victory that had invigorated even us four grade grubbers.

"She was a crazy woman, really, though, wasn't she," said Henry, meaning it affectionately, Anna, fearless now after your decade-long absence. Malcolm lit two candles in stubby silver candlesticks considerably tarnished from years in the back of his mother's china cupboard. "I am a mystery: kindle my flame," he intoned, quoting, as we often did, the graduation poem you wrote us, two lines here or one there, because it was our common property, our bond. Then he clicked off the ceiling light.

The flames bathed our faces honey gold, and we seemed our younger selves for an instant. "Yes, she was a crazy woman. How did we ever survive her?" Malcolm wondered. "And why can't we get rid of her even now?" asked Henry. And then, spooning our host's surprisingly hot chili into old chowder bowls familiar from Saturday lunches as Malcolm's best friend, the young baritone, recently of the Saarbrücken Opera, told us how you'd haunted him all across your old Europe. "Everything I did," he said, "I felt her watching. In a museum, in a palace, in a cathedral, even in a garden. And when I sang, from the first row, those wide eyes watching — I had to sing my best for them, or not so much sing my best, maybe, because the notes themselves never mattered much to Aylmer, but get the character right, through the words. Schaunard in *Bohème*, Arlecchino in *Ariadne*, not bad parts — of course, I had my share of first shepherds and second knights, but I always felt I had to, what, find the precise inflection, the truth of it? Remember when she'd interrupt us if she heard us reading only the words, not what was behind them?"

We all heard you then, Anna, echoing in our heads through red wine and candlelight: *Oh but, Kinder, you are not puppets, please. Yammer yammer yammer — I cannot bear to hear it. You must understand and read, all in one breath, as if your life depends on it. Life is at the moment, nicht? What other possible time is it?*

"Stupid me, I was figuring we were free of her," Kip muttered, tucking an unruly black lock back into his headband. But we decided that, after all, we were indeed free, weren't we? From a single context, bound by you and Quissick, we had found our separate ways into the world. And now it was, perhaps, the converging electrical force fields of four brains, each inscribed with a myriad squiggles that signified Anna Aylmer, which caused your voice to resound again as if out loud, as if still speaking to us. *I shall be hovering, drawing you here.* Yes, it was as you'd prophesied in your poem, that sly aping of the last stanza in *Faust* (see, we recognized it, Anna: you'd taught us well). We should not have been surprised to find you circling around us.

"But how crazy was she?" Rupert, always the quietest,

finally said, barely pausing from shoveling spoonfuls of red glop into his mouth as if he hadn't eaten in days. "Pass the sour cream, Phipps," he added to deflect any immediate answer. We all pondered. "Was she as crazy as my aunt, for instance?" he proposed. "Or my uncle?" said Malcolm. "Was she as crazy as Lucia di Lammermoor?" said Henry, who had lined up an audition for a Donizetti festival in Rhode Island.

You'll be glad to learn that Kip said he didn't think you were crazy at all. It was something else. You were possessed with a mission, as you always had been. What sort of woman in her thirties, with two teenage daughters, trucked herself off to Spain to fight on the losing side? What sort cast off husbands and lovers and abandoned her girls then resurfaced in a New Hampshire pond, hanging around with a gang of reds from the University of Chicago? Whoever would hunker down in a decomposing town like Quissick, Massachusetts, and live above a greasy luncheonette in the warehouse district by the train yards and lie abed (we imagined) with piles of books on her bed table reading late into the night, every lonely night, as the railroad cars were shunted and switched and finally the factory bells began to sound when she had only just nodded off? Or did she ever sleep? Did she wake like an owl, with two bright eyes darting across pages and pages of their only sustenance — words — and with ears pricked to catch the subtlest nuance in the voice from her phonograph singing her a night song, no doubt in German and on a crackling overplayed record from the public library, *A Winter Journey, A Poet's Love?* Did she think occasionally of her four boys, her Bohemians in training, her harlequin

quartet of youth and hope, and make plans for them? Were
they her newest mission? Or was she still, as Abraham
Phipps seemed convinced, an international spy of some
stripe, hiding out in a most unlikely spot where she could
accomplish her subversion unsuspected? Or perhaps she'd
been put out to pasture now that her usefulness had ex-
pired. Had there seemed, in fact, all that much difference,
in the Quissick of those days, between un-American politics and un-American aesthetics? Whose culture really
claimed her? That she was unacquainted with the func-
tion of the purple-and-white pom-pom was enough to
make her somewhat suspect. That she belonged to no
church, not even the Unitarian on Station Street, that she
braided her hair and bound it atop her head in such a foreign manner, that her dresses were so severe, so black and
brown and gray, that she expected even someone like Cato
Skerritt to take his Spanish lessons as seriously as if he actually wanted to learn the language — all these things
were commented on. "Who does that bag think she is!"
Cato used to fume at the dinner table, unaware how the
sentiment echoed Kip's own when he was prodded to out-
perform himself. Kip heard the similarity only later; at the
time, he'd figured what you expected of your chosen four
had no equivalent in the stretch required of his goof-off
brother.

But we all admitted, as we approached thirty, that you
alone, Anna, had forced us up against the unknown. A
Spanish verb (peleaba, quedado) might well have proved
Cato's nemesis, but we had limits too, and you insisted we
assault them. That was why you seemed so crazy. No one
else in our upbringing had presented study as quite such

an ever-expanding field, finally boundless, no end to what we might find there. It was crazy-making, and so we called you crazy. How could we satisfy you, how could we be the good students we'd worked so hard to be? You always wanted something more, the next, the more difficult. A fleeting acknowledgment that, yes, this is a true sentence, that, ah, you have understood, children, and then on! At times we felt you were leading us to a precipice. In Malcolm's apartment after ten years without you, we decided that in a certain sense you had been doing just that. But the precipice was yours, not ours, and you didn't expect us to follow you over it. You only wanted to nudge us up to the brink, Anna, and leave us trembling there in our own anticipation.

*Here: look, think, feel, listen, do. Have you not had enough sleep, dear ones? Is that all it is? But wake up, muchachos. Look at what is before you.*

It had proved impossible for us four to coexist without you. When we were gathered together, you, even a decade in the grave, were always with us.

As you are now.

Or, at least, you're on your way to us. We sense you sailing over these Atlantic waves like a discoverer of new worlds. *Where are my four boys now?* Well, they haven't been there just beyond the iron balustrade of that old New England cemetery in which you lie. Not lately. You don't sense their spirits even in the county beyond. They're addressing you, not from the east, not from Boston where once they reassembled themselves like pieces of a treasure map. That comforted you, the regenerated fourfold message received after their Wanderjahre. But its electric

charge had been obscured soon again by static distur-
bances in the spirit world you inhabit, and you discerned
only intermittently your Kip's signal faint amongst the
burble of academics, the soft low buzz of your Ru, hardly
even a whisper of your hardworking Malcolm, and only an
occasional sudden baritone blast of your Henry, then gone
again. And so why now? All together somewhere, and in-
tensely concentrating on you, on our perpetual communion. *It blows from the south. Over water. A warmer
wind. I must go.*

The part of you that exists still, invisibly, must have already begun the journey, Anna, because each day, each
hour we meditate on you, we find you nearer. Are we
drawing you — to life? How close in tight you drew us
then, held us, wouldn't let us go, and now we're invoking
that power for ourselves, because we need you here as
close as once you needed us. Is it age that teaches us this?
Whatever did we think we really needed, soul-deep and till
death, back when you knew us in the flesh? Muchachos do
not conceive existence in such impermanent terms. But
you, who had questioned the permanence even of half the
globe, knew better than to let us slip through your fingers.
Sift us, yes, but catch us in the other hand, hand over
hand, turn us lovingly and sift again, catch and sift, a ped-
agogic hourglass, instructing us to notice what flies past,
to take account, to contemplate. But never to let us go. Because, in your life, so much had already gone, such em-
pires, such lovers, such daughters, and what might you
ever have the chance again to grasp so firmly and forever?
These shall be my progeny, you may have said, to bide
with me into old age.

But you didn't wait for age, did you, Anna? Could you not trust us enough? Could you not have stood to watch us disappearing from you in our casual American fashion as we surely would? You didn't credit your own power, Señora Aylmer. Come, look at us now, and find some comfort again.

Kip is leaning over against Rupert in the easy posture of a football player on the bench. You might think nothing of it, find no evidence of the years of impossible wrangling between two people who love each other and fear each other in equal measure. That Malcolm's flickering eye every half minute inspects them in their comradely pose might indicate nothing more than his habitual jitteriness, reassuring himself that all is well. Or is it? Henry's mind's on something more potent, the recent death of his friend Ledyard, whose requiem he sang as we have told you. We're each stunned, at odd times, by this instance of a death too young. Your own was young enough, Anna, and how often it still stuns us, your death itself, but always accompanied by your hovering spirit; with Ledyard, as yet, there is no presence but swift death to contemplate. Henry knew him best and first and brought his friendship to all of us; though they were but passing lovers, it is Henry, naturally, who misses him most.

*But then why are you wasting such feeling on me, mes enfants? If you have just lost your comrade? Why are you drawing me to you over the water? Draw him instead, think of him, children.*

But you help us consider death, Anna, because it was the last thing you taught us. We are not ready to draw Ledyard back to us.

It is evening now again. We are still at the table on the veranda. It would be silent here but for the steadily crashing waves, no birdsongs now after dark. It is nearly the last week of the calendar, and so warm. We have finished off the meal with christophenes. We'll leave you one on your jumbie table so you may taste something rare and luscious after the fish and plantain and breadfruit.

We are reluctant to rise from our chairs. How often the four of us have sat about a table together. It is possible the day is coming when only three of us may sit together, and which three will they be, Anna? *Ach, amigos, that is it at last. Yes, you have begun to see what I have seen. It is suddenly more serious, isn't it? Now you will truly begin to read as you have not read before. It is no more to pass time, not even to enrich time, children, but to save yourselves from time. All stories are about time, have I not told you this? They are how we master it.* And as we are mulling this over, you leap to your next thought, specifying in teacherly fashion as always, leading us where you want us to go: *But suddenly I am thinking, dear ones, of the famous story by Clifford Skerritt, the story of the impending collision. I am sure you have not forgotten* . . .

Ah yes, Kip's great project, which you dragged out of him page by agonizing page. If Henry spoke sense in his papers, Kip could only go roundabout; sense was not a large enough mystery for him. "Can I write a creative paper instead?" he'd asked. You told us everything must be creative in your class. "But I mean a story. I can't write an essay." *No, we shall leave the essay to Malcolm Phipps, is that it? And you, my friend, you must write what only you must write, and then we shall see what it comes to.*

A frightening prospect, but you meant it perfectly naturally. What else did you ever expect, after all, but to see what we could do? Kip, however, took it as a challenge that he must now prove his artistry. The imitation Kerouac had to go. You were tiring of it, and it no longer satisfied him either, truth be told. After a protracted struggle, that other contemporary American, Vladimir Vladimirovich Nabokov, was taking the upper hand. But how could Kip Skerritt presume to imitate his new demigod? His scrawled attempts choked themselves to death in a tangle of subordinate clauses. There must be a middle path that was his own. He kept eliciting his friends' advice, dawdling in the corridors between classes, swinging with Rupert head to toe in his backyard hammock while the maple leaves fell around, or late evenings snacking up at the Vigneaults'. "How's this for an approach?" he'd say, and the others would invariably declare it might work but, Kip, sooner or later you'll have to finish the damn thing. Even Rupert had almost finished his, and that was unprecedented.

Kip was in a crisis. He'd imagined this paper had to be the sign of not only promise but arrival. He knew Henry had, in a sense, arrived somewhere ahead of him. But Henry's art did not come entirely from inside him, he hadn't composed those songs he sang. His was more like a talent for sport, a gift, an aptitude, while Kip had to hack away at a granite block, he told himself, and hew from it something no one had ever seen before. Who would instruct him to take a breath here, to sustain a phrase just so? He was alone. The rest of us weren't too keen on this new pretension, but you didn't seem to mind it, Anna. The preparatory speculation, naturally, you'd cut short, but the agonizing? There you honored him. *I have new respect for my beatnik,* you proclaimed when he brought in his bursting folder of false starts and fragments. *Take an extra week, or two if you must. These deadlines are somewhat arbitrary, child.* "Now you tell us," grumbled Rupert, who had finally managed to hand something in on time.

"I'm under way at last," Kip had reported the Saturday before in his own family's kitchen, where the four of us had gathered after yet another football afternoon. "Glory be," Henry sighed. But Kip wasn't going to head upstairs to work quite yet. He needed to simmer awhile.

Though the final product, weeks later, had a certain originality and was surely as remarkable a piece as any Quissick high schooler churned out that year, or any other year most likely, and though it impressively took up a full third of one issue of the *Quiddity* (editor: C. Skerritt), it was only when Kip first improvised on his themes for his three pals around the kitchen table that the famous story of the collision, Anna, seemed to be already as great as its author yearned for it to be.

It took place in Colorado, a place Kip had never been. He had to invent his own Rockies, so he thought of a Skerritt family expedition into the White Mountains of New Hampshire and of his dad's terror on the gravel roads, the hairpins, and how he, Kip, had lain on the floor of the station wagon unwilling to look out though Cato and Io kept calling him a fairy. You two want to get barfed on? he'd threatened, but they'd only squealed and made their father even more nervous up front next to breath-holding Mom and the nursing twins. (Babies no longer ride in front seats, Anna. In many respects, it is a more cautious world than the one you knew.)

None of this family stuff appeared in his story, of course, just the crunching gravel and the sense of a fragile shallop riding a miraculous ever-ascending wave, cresting only to keep rising. Its passengers felt an evident vacuum at the roofs of their stomachs. Kip was sure about that: in the White Mountains it was decidedly the roof that had felt so void, not the much-maligned pit; his stomach had been a cavern, half full of muck, and the bare walls of its over-arching vault had ached in the emptiness. He'd never forgotten it. But who was it driving up Kip's imaginary Rockies? On page two, they emerged as a middle-aged couple, Russian émigrés apparently, with wistful thoughts of Chekhov's journey across Siberia, of Tolstoy in the Caucasus, episodes young Kip had only slight knowledge of but managed to invoke obliquely so as not to reveal his ignorance. And what were such literary Old World folk doing heading for Independence Pass? The gentleman, it seemed, was a butterfly hunter, and in the evenings and on cloudy days he was also a species of novelist; the lady quite tolerated his pursuits and cheerfully typed his manuscripts and assisted in cataloging the lepidoptera. We find them an admirable pair, we're amused by their fascination with American tourist courts and roadside eateries and place names.

We didn't tell him so, but as Kip portrayed them we knew they were his parents idealized. They were two together, with all of art and nature, and their one son was away at summer camp, perhaps, and no other children cluttered the frame. They did not drift off into the newspaper or the kitchen radio; they did not squabble or screech. Through years of dislocation, they were home and hearth to each other. Peace accompanied them, even in a strange landscape. Their rattling old station wagon held a high pile of luggage surmounted by a butterfly net, ever ready for the chase. She drove, he watched. It was a slow ascent, but sure.

And for all the impression of endless upwardness, there would eventually come a final crest, the pass itself, where unknown to the Russians another rattletrap car, a big Hudson, had just appeared from the other direction. It was jammed full of young drifters, six or seven of them — it was hard to tell, what with heads in laps and feet out windows. They had a game going; they were about to coast down the mountain. Here's where the pit of the stomach came into play; it was a different feeling, the wild descent. Without gas, scarcely with brakes, the man at the wheel was set to fly. Beyond the half-naked girl nuzzling up to his side sat a somewhat less free-spirited fellow, elbow hanging out the window — casual or bracing for dear life? He'd never learned how to drive, but he'd spent more of the past few years on the road than sitting still. In the trunk there was a duffel full of the bundles of word-littered paper he'd carried with him everywhere. Words, to him, were as much landscape as those mountains. The roaring ride down from the pass was like a tumble of unstoppable prose, gobbling the air around him.

And then, around the Skerritt kitchen table with its huge Philco radio and plastic yellow mats and gas-station glassware and bright orange cloth napkins in rings shaped like each kid's totem — Kip's a horse, Cato's a shark — the budding author explained how he would return to the station wagon and its thoughtful conversation, then back again to the careening Hudson, whooping and hollering, and his readers would begin to realize that two great American novels are taking shape, right then, in those very vehicles.

"Literary criticism in story form," said Kip with some ten years' perspective when, in Malcolm's little studio apartment, we'd moved the table back to a corner and three of us had sunk onto the daybed, leaving Rupert absentmindedly tipping back against the desk in the sturdiest of chairs. "I was ahead of the style. Metafiction they'd call it now, right, Ru?" "Who knows." "But I kept waiting for the crash," said Henry, who'd stretched back on the pillows, almost asleep he seemed. "But the crash wasn't the point. I was on to something essential about American literature, see, Henry. Besides, if you want to know, they swerved at the last moment and went home to write *Lolita* and *On the Road*." "But it got so vague and cataclysmic," Henry recalled from his stupor. "Well, Aylmer wasn't too pleased with the ending either," Kip admitted, "but I wanted it open to interpretation. That's what I thought literature was for." It was as if we could all suddenly hear your voice, Anna, fairly booming across our classroom again: *But, my friends, literature is eventually not so imprecise. It has many meanings, yes, dear ones, but they are precise ones. You are still boys. So it is maybe better not to look too hard yet. You enjoy the great impenetrable fog, is that it? Ja, vielleicht . . .* Your thought trailed off, and we watched you behind your desk musing on mysteries we hadn't yet proved ready to approach with you, as close as you'd tried to bring us to them.

But you let it be. When Kip's story appeared in the literary magazine you smiled and told him yes, you'd read it again, yes, it did look quite fine set in type, and indeed there were some passages he should be rather pleased with. *Passages only, Comrade Skerritt, but still, a passage, a sentence, sometimes even one word is an achievement.* Kip immediately wanted to know which passages. *Oh, perhaps the suddenly shining red hood of the car of beatniks when the sun peeks between clouds, how it flashes, far away, like a butterfly on the mountainside. Perhaps the dust in the Russian lady's rearview mirror pluming into Tartar horsemen in pursuit. But not the ending, no, child, you have not solved the problem you set before you. A storyteller is a kind of scientist, I would say. You have not yet the rigor in your method.*

Kip tried not to look too crestfallen. He made another approach to keep you talking about his work: "So is my story about time, like you said all stories are? I don't really see what it has to do with time." *But think, muchacho. Is it not a clock you have set ticking? It is a time bomb, you might even say. These curves, these velocities —* "And that's why I wanted it to end before the actual crash, to keep that metaphor . . ." *No, but because the crash is still inside you, my dear one. These Nabokovs and Kerouacs, they live with you, and one must not yet destroy the other, though you wish it also perhaps a little, for life would then be a bit clearer. But soon will come more books to confuse you even further. And you will wonder who you are and how you belong anywhere at all. The crash is real. American literature is the metaphor, child. You have it backwards. The artist keeps eyes clear. Perhaps you need see only one more thing. A story may end in a sentence.* Oh, Frau Aylmer, thought Kip then amongst his friends in the candlelight (one candle on the windowsill over Beacon Street, one on the desk behind Rupert), that artist you tried to breathe into me — no, I'm a scholar, after all, like you. Like you, Anna. It turns out I've wanted to be you ever since you first found me.

Kip knew, then, how in everything you'd done, in your severest criticism, you'd been showing him how to become a teacher. With his finger he hooked the glass ring of the jug on the floor by his feet and poured himself some more wine. *All through your history, utter my name* was echoing in his head, so he spoke the lines aloud to his friends.

"But the thing Aylmer missed," said Rupert suddenly, sitting, as he was, higher than the rest slumping on Malcolm's daybed. He paused for effect. That muffled look of his had fallen away; he had devilish lights in his eyes. Even Henry sat up a bit to catch what Rupert was going to say. Malcolm looked apprehensive. Kip was raising an eyebrow to ward off some uncomfortable revelation, and Rupert seemed pleased to have everyone's attention. His close-mouthed approach to life gave weight to these rare pronouncements. "Well, but ten years ago, who could really talk about sex, even Aylmer! But it definitely wasn't books that got Kip so confused. Kip handled any book you threw at him. It was us having sex all the time, and no one knowing — that was the collision coming up around the bend in that damn story. If you ask me." "And you were just Joe Cool," snapped Kip.

Henry had opened his eyes wide, but Malcolm was staring at the floor. "Yeah, pretty cool, anyway," said Rupert. "I wasn't having guilt fits. I wasn't worrying about my future family life. I wasn't afraid how abnormal I was." "You were abnormal to start with," said Henry. "Right. I liked doing things that didn't fit. Kip only half did. And, boy, did he like that half. But then he'd freak. You two thought I was the wreck. Should've seen him after a session in bed!" "Spare us the details," said Malcolm, and we'll spare you them, too, Anna. We can't imagine you hearing these things.

But Rupert went on. He said too much. He was tired of being dumped on for not eating regularly, not dressing decently, not having any real job or home or plan. He knew he had his own kind of sanity that Kip didn't. He had an immediate sense of the bare bones of life, of what he wanted right then and needed and managed to get, while Kip flailed — what to do a thesis on, whether to go on in psychotherapy, if he should keep seeing Rupert because it drove him nuts but then he was nuts when he didn't see him. With his long hair and headband and ponytail and, now that it was spring, shorts and sandals. Kip fit right into his Cambridgeport world of seventh-year grad students and counterculture intellectuals, indecisive, perpetually self-analyzing. But Rupert had decided: he would have as much sex as he possibly could; he would read whatever he wanted to, volume after volume; he would not attach himself to anything, not even to a routine; he would get up and go out whenever he felt like it and keep most of his thoughts to himself. For a meager income, he collected and sold old books on street corners or in parks where other people sold jewelry or T-shirts. He lived cheap in his South End flophouse. He saw Kip once or twice a week, but Kip couldn't call him because he never had a phone. It was always best with Kip because they knew each other so well — that he admitted. If Kip would only accept being a fag (a new proud word then, Anna) and see what a fun subversive thing it was not to have to sit tight on your rear end like a man. But when Rupert got talking that way, it made Kip feel shaky inside. And right then, seeing Kip's face go all crooked, Rupert knew he was tormenting his friend yet again, and publicly this time, and he'd better stop.

Malcolm had slipped off into the kitchen alcove to wash the dishes. "So anyway," Rupert said, looking hard at Henry but speaking quietly now, mostly to himself, "what I'm getting at is that Kip and I can't live together. That's why I'm moving in with you instead." And Kip, subdued, cautioned: "Are you sure you're ready for him, Henry?"

"Henry, I'm glad you're back in town to take these two off my hands," came the tired voice of Malcolm over the splashing in the sink.

And there we were, Anna, four of us, beginning our next period of entanglement. Is this not at all how you'd hoped to see us by then? *Now come, Kinder, surely you have by now discovered that adult life is not always so grown up. Are you smiling at us, Anna? At our unsteadiness? But, dear ones, I, too, had my several loves.*

T HEN we'll continue.

To himself, secretly, Malcolm had admitted he felt finally comfortable again with these friends of his, squabbles and all. It was somehow relaxing, relieving to have no feminine component present; Malcolm didn't feel he had to be so much in charge, so responsible. His old cranky cautiousness must have been what Rupert meant by men sitting tight and all that. This homosexuality of theirs seemed to allow them to step aside from the fierce world. Was that shameful? Yes, but also rather fascinating to Malcolm. He couldn't escape a sense of high school revived, the last time he'd felt fully at home, fully safe; all that mattered to him then was his friends. He'd loved each of them, he'd never imagined being apart from them for long — even when they were cross with him. Odd: ever since the war began, men themselves hadn't seemed quite the same to Malcolm, being a man hadn't seemed quite the same. Every night, those sad faces of soldiers on television, those faces younger than his own. Yes, ever since the war — *Mes amis, please stop! It is too much. You are telling me of Malcolm but you are speaking also of this war. No, but don't tell me of another war! Did Europe finally blow itself up? I cannot bear it, children!*

But hadn't you sensed around you, Anna, the weeping families standing by new graves not far from where you lay? Hadn't you yet encountered in your spirit world old students you'd known and cared for, students you'd taught Spanish to? Quissick sent its share, and because it was a poor man's war Upper and Lower Quiddy and Tunxet Village more than Tunxet Farms or Opossum Hill. Cato Skerritt did sign right up and two years later came home safe, but Andrew Idlenot died, and boys from the hog farms and boys from the tenements . . .

Kip and Rupert had their easy out, of course, a strange form of privilege that Kip finally shied from invoking since he had a student deferment anyway. Henry's family doctor bestowed a history of bronchial asthma on the deep-breathing baritone, but Malcolm really did have the flattest of feet, though he claimed he would have gone C.O. — besides, by then he was a father. (The rest of us could hardly conceive of Martha Hooper let alone Louisa and little Anna, still too young to come stay with their dad, known to him at that stage only through awkward motel meetings for which he flew out to California.)

No, we really have nothing to tell you of that war, Anna. You've lain in the bleeding earth closer to it than we have. Only recently, curiously, from an unlikely quarter, have we begun to feel what it may have been like for young men to watch comrades die for nothing and suffer their countrymen's scorn. When it was over, Anna, that war brought back to Quissick, along a trail of wounded bodies and souls, the Vongpranith Convenience and Oriental Market and our very own Buddhist temple over on Church Street. Does that tell you enough?

*Then Europe has not again lost its mind.*

Ah, Anna, your Europe is as crazy as it's always been. Your two Berlins still glare at each other. There are so many missiles poised for flight there might as well be only a single inevitable one. Does the rent in your native soil seem reassuringly familiar? Not everything has changed in twenty-five years, after all.

*So, children, you are acquainted now firsthand with history. Yes, I hear it in your sadder voices. You boys — I call you boys still, I cannot help it — you have lived already long enough to tell what has changed and what has not. The last is more important, perhaps. You are now each of you maybe a nervy spine that runs through time. Your own past, whatever you can know of it, it holds you up, encases you — yes? But always it is melting away. As you burn on, it drips, it cracks and topples off. It, at the last, may seem candle wax merely. Was that not how I once put it to you?*

Wax, wick, flame. We have been trying for your sake, Anna Aylmer, to render our past back to you, clarified, as we know it now, as it drops like melting wax away from us. In the poem you said that we must keep your flame kindled, that we must not forget, that you are always before us, drawing us to you. But you are also our past, Anna. What is your poem's precise meaning? We have decided to write it out tonight so we may leave it on the jumbie table for you as our spell to conjure with.

And now we hear you chortling an embarrassed awkward

laugh, and your warm reassurance whispers across time to us, your pupils: *Each wick is dear.* Yes, we'll still be your wicks, you our flame. But come to us, teach us what mystery still abides in that beacon flame of yours.

We see you now in the old classroom. Suddenly, we're seniors again. It's winter weather outside, Christmas is near. Soon you will take your brief solitude again between semesters. You'll perch owl-like, in your rooms above the luncheonette and fall into one of your open-eyed trances. We imagine thoughts swirling around your hibernation like the swirling of December snow. You'll be a vortex of thought, a source and receptacle at once.

But now in the classroom still, we watch you as closely as you watch us. Here we see only your daylight incarnation, the worn old brown suit with the amber brooch, the pepper and salt braid tightly bound atop your gray brow, the big blue-gray eyes investigating us. In our second year with you, it is no more relaxed. We are still on edge. But we've come to long for that quality of nervousness. We get it three times a week now, MWF instead of TT on our weekly schedules.

You are speaking: *I have something to propose that I have not proposed before.*

That is the case every class, of course, but anticipating the Christmas break we sense something ominous in your words. What will you be expecting of us now?

*We have only six months more with each other, mes enfants. And I do not know that we are anywhere further along than when we started. I, too, am struck at times with despair, you see. Is it possible? A teacher despairs? Certainly our parents despair, you will say, and our crazy aunt and our crazy uncle. Certainly our parents also give up on us. And we don't mind giving up on them either, now that we are so tall and strong and ready to leave them behind.* We're narrowing our eyes and feeling a chill from the rattling frames of the big windows at the end of the classroom. Is some terrible reprimand coming? Can we withstand it? We imagine running across ice patches on sidewalk after sidewalk to Rupert's welcome refuge where we may consolidate ourselves after the storm that is surely about to come from those frowning lips across the wide cluttered desktop.

*Children!* You startle our nerves. The awkward way you pace your voice — a bark, an interminable pause, a rushed phrase, a visible struggle for the right word, then a complicated paragraph all at once — no other teacher talks the way you do. Even Monsieur Simone's inaccurate English is easier to listen to. *Have you yet — but no. Ach, where is that damned thing?* Now you're assaulting a stack of books, lifting from the top and pulling out from beneath and not finding what you're looking for. The stack rocks perilously. Then you catch sight of something green peeking from under a pile of blue books, the Spanish II exams probably, and your hand grabs for it as for a treasure. And now comes the riffling of pages, the nearsighted squinting up and down. Then, suddenly, you stand, scraping the chair leg on the much-scraped linoleum and, no longer a mere bust behind your desk, appear full-length before us. We are aware of your old lady shoes, the thick cubes of your heels, the trim laces — black shoes, not brown like your suit — and your heavy stockings that give no sense of skin underneath. Your left hand with its purple agate set in gold clutches the rim of the desk to steady you as you begin to read to us, as if they were your own words, softly spoken: *"He there does now enjoy eternall rest and happy ease, which thou doest want and crave, and further from it daily wanderest . . ."* This is Despair speaking, children. I mean it literally. We are in an allegory. I am afraid you do not know yet **The Faerie Queene.** Mr. Davenport might find it perhaps a bit more daunting than even his whales. *"What if some little payne the passage have, that makes frayle flesh to feare the bitter wave? . . ."* You hear? This is enormously seducing, dear ones. *"Is not short payne well borne, that brings long ease, and layes the soule to sleepe in quiet grave?"* Just listen to the sounds now. Sounds only, no meaning. And you speak now as if hypnotizing us, drawing out vowels like moans and sighs. *"Sleepe after toyle, port after stormie seas, ease after warre, death after life, does greatly please."* Hear it? These are famous English lines, Kinder, and it is an honor to have you learn Spenser first from my old German mouth. Forgive me. Your language can sound very beautiful.

And, gulping to hold back a trembling in your breast, you read the last couplet again and make us savor it now in our own mouths. And now you're writing the nine lines in their quaint spellings on the board and making us each in turn read aloud to show how the words move us still, again and again. We imagine we'll be reading the entire poem — oh no, there's a second volume you're brandishing now — over our Christmas vacation. But that fear proves false.

*Now you know it is there,* you say. *Someday that single stanza ringing in your memory will draw you back to these little green books. They shall be in the library wait-ing for each of you.* Reprieved. But you do want us to fol-low you, now, in the meditation you've begun on that voice of despair whispering inside our mortal heads. *You do not hear it yet, children? It is there even in you. I hear it always. It informs me that I may leave you all, that I may not return in the new year, that I may abandon this town. What is to hold me? And what is to hold you, dear ones? Have you never heard that question in the silence of night?* We say nothing, watch you stand there, frail, unac-countably old now. *I have left many times,* you say, *but twice already have I left something all too dear. Yes, I have left Germany, I have left Spain, but what have I left there? My children did not survive the wars. I tell you this now so you will know from what depth my despair speaks to me. No, it is not you, boys, you do not disappoint me. It is not you who are no further along. You grow, you learn. But despair tells me that there is so much thinking and what does it bring but sorrow to us who have followed our thought so long and far? Perhaps I should not think, not teach you thinking. Perhaps sleep is better, you see.*

You are moving slowly back around your desk, touching it to support yourself as if you really might collapse. We have never heard such words from you, such limping faint-ing tones. Henry, possessed of some courtliness drilled into him by his mother, steps up to you, gently, with arm extended, and to our surprise you clasp it tightly and allow him to help you settle back into your chair.

Do you remember all this, Anna, or were you then too deep in your trance to notice anything around you? That's how it seemed: as if we'd been allowed to attend your spirit in its utter weakness. It was not such intimacy as we'd hoped for. We'd recognized your loneliness, Anna, but we imagined you staunch in the face of it. And there you sat, as if crushed, beneath that stanza in white chalk, the letters bearing traces of the gothic shapes your small hand had learned before the First World War.

Or had it all been a performance for us? Forgive us, we could not discount the notion then. Had you been impersonating Despair for us? A vivid lesson. Had you thought that morning, *Um Gottes Willen, we have been too noble this semester. I must make them feel what it is to give it all up. They are too American to confess such yearnings. But I am teaching the soul not the good intentions. I must shake them. Perhaps if I appear to be faltering, to have not spirit enough left . . .*

We should have known you would never be so calculating, Anna. Your lessons were always as true for you as for us. It could not have been otherwise. The picture of you at your desk, alone, dimly illuminated the background of our thoughts over that Christmas. It accompanied our reading, our time wasting, our family interplay, our yearning, and indeed we touched upon something of your despair inside us, despite our healthy young selves.

It is Christmas now again. We know more of that despair now, Anna, but still nothing we know has seemed quite equal to yours. Will we not let ourselves take it as deep as you? You, in our present time, might once more say to hell with this old world we cling to still.

The stars are out. The waves crash. There are the carols of a church choir fading in and out along the hillside above us. "God bless the master of this house, the mistress also . . ." We wonder, for a moment, where, really, we are in this soft summery breeze. Our silent faces regard each other across the cleared table. Malcolm is thinking, like you, of his children who are not here with him, Henry of his dear dead friend Ledyard, Kip and Rupert of their tumult and their compromise, and all of us of a specter of death, which, with your ghost, may also be winging toward us through space and time. But maybe not yet, Anna, please, may it be not yet.

PART TWO

# Visitation

A SPECTER of death also winging toward you, dear ones? But I think it is I alone on this breeze that warms me more with each mile, as if I were coming back into life. You imagine death is also on its way, children?

No. It is surely only Anna Aylmer. You remember me as I was and as I will be as long as you live.

Now I hear those carols too. There, deep in the palms. You do not recall, maybe, how the four of you came one winter night and stood beneath my window in the dim light of my streetlamp and sang a strange harmony to me — which was the song? "Es ist ein Ros' entsprungen" — yes? Henry's voice at least sang forth true, and I could hear Malcolm almost with the melody. A tender Christmas present to the old teacher in her last December. I see you down there in my street, lamplight reflecting up from the snow to your soft young faces. Let me see you like that again now. I am almost there.

I shall fill this space around you and find you and hold you all again. You have summoned me, dearest ones. But you will not feel me quite yet. You must keep imagining me. I will watch awhile till the time comes to tell you something I never told you in life.

But I told you already so much, did I not?

I told you more than anyone has ever told you. I am immodest. Yes, I know.

Light from an open door.

A dozen black women, ah, and a black man or two, and a handful of children, all dressed for church, out caroling in the English manner. "Among the leaves so green . . ." And now four dark shapes in the doorway.

My boys!

Light shines out on the singing faces. In silhouette my waiting boys shift awkwardly. I have spotted each of them at once: Kip leans casually, my skinny Rupert slouches, Henry upright as if to go onstage, and with folded hands and head shyly bowed Malcolm. So they stood once at the door of my classroom or down on the street in Riverbend as I leaned out and babbled fondly, "Oh, dear ones, you do not forget your Señora," and would have called them all upstairs, brought them in from the cold to my nest had I thought to tidy the place or had something on hand besides strong coffee, something sweet for the holiday in my miserable larder. "If I had known to expect you, mes enfants." And still they smiled and shook their heads no, they did not want to intrude, only to cheer me for a moment with their lopsided quartet — how they must have practiced!

"Amid the cold of winter, when half-spent was the night . . ." So it goes in English, they told me when the new year brought us back to Quissick High, and in my classroom with those white globes hung high on the ceiling glowing faintly yellow, hardly adding light to the January afternoon, there we sat, remembering their song. But they would not sing it again, they would only listen to me talk about the lovely words and how in both languages they sounded beautiful. Why is it I still think of my boys together always with beautiful language? Well, it was my mission. Jerry Davenport had no notion of language. He could teach them *Moby-Dick* as a matter only of information. But you must take a small child and squeeze its little shoulder and from birth whisper into its ear, like a ghost, maybe, until words sound through to the soul.

*I'm afraid there's no mistress here,* comes a voice. It is Malcolm's, somewhat cautious. These people have called forth blessings on the master of the house, the mistress also, but here they find only masters — four of them. Everyone is nervously laughing. "But you have girlfriends at home?" says a very large woman holding out a basket from which dangle shell necklaces and earrings and ribbons with beads on them. And my dear ones consult each other. Henry steps away to return soon with paper money in his palm, which he counts out — I see faces of the British queen, one, two, three of them. The carolers seem pleased, and from the basket it is Kip who draws a long pearly chain and Malcolm two pairs of amber baubles. *For my daughters,* he says. This seems to relieve the large woman. He has daughters — then perhaps it is not so strange to find here in our upstanding parish these four white men alone with themselves. Happy Christmas, they all now say and sing another of their carols, about the leaf of the green maple tree, moving on up the dirt road into darkness. Why do they sing like this at night on this island? Is it to charm the tourist and sell their wares, or has the Old World despite its cruelties in some magic fashion penetrated their hearts too? My boys ponder this question with the door now closed and the song fading up the hill.

I have entered. I am here.

This Professor Howard they have spoken of, he keeps a spare household. Perhaps he is as modest as I, a table, a couple of chairs, a bed for restless sleep. This place is like a new bungalow in Tunxet Farms but with wooden shutters for window glass. A straw mat, cane furniture with once-blue cushions pale from being hauled onto the veranda in the sun, I can tell. This is where anyone might live, no touch of Professor Howard himself, a foothold merely in his land of birth. I never kept such a remnant: my old world was gone. True, in the early fifties, I did take some of Quissick's wealthy daughters to see my Europe, but England, France, and Italy only, never Germany, never Spain. Did my boys hear tell of those travels, the much divorced Frau Aylmer and three summers of girls under her wing? I could not have taken boys, much as I would rather have. Ah, but I did tell Henry when we talked of the tour he one day hoped to make for himself; I told him how one of my charges had gasped at her first sight of the *David*, loud enough to turn Florentine heads —"My God, Señora, to have a date with a man like that!" It startled Henry that I told him such a tale. There he sits in this shadowy room, reddening to think of it. My memory has invaded his. It is the rule of ghosts: just as my boys' collective call roused me from the suspension in which I may barely be said to exist, so my meditations now penetrate theirs. Henry, look up. He does, at the bulb hung from the ceiling within a wicker ball. It casts strange dark shapes on the bare whitewashed walls.

Kip, playfully, is looping his purchase, the long necklace of shells, twice around Rupert's thin neck. Rupert allows him to do so. They are as I always saw them, but no longer furtive. They do not know how I used to catch Kip's soft glances, the constant inclining toward his diffident friend, nor caught Rupert's beckoning, the swing of his shoulders, the cocked hip, the saunter, the lassitude. And, of course, I perceived Kip's agonies and Rupert's terror. They do not know I always knew them. Only I did not imagine they would still be able to touch each other so tenderly after so many years. They have been luckier than I.

Now Rupert on the straw mat leans back against Kip's knees. He does not mind having this necklace, he likes how it droops across the strange words in red on his white T-shirt: MISS ROYAL INTER-ISLAND TALENTED TEEN PAGEANT '87.

But it is Malcolm still speaking. *And why is their custom closer to my custom than anything I ever knew?* "We are not daily beggars who go from door to door, we are your neighbors' children whom you have seen before." *That's my custom, not theirs. But they have the words for it still.*

*They'll forget them in another generation,* says Henry, sure of it.

*Because the custom becomes a tradition,* says Kip, *and tradition becomes only an enactment of a custom until it ends up as something known only to anthropologists. But as Anna might say, books don't die off like that.* Kip's hands are kneading Rupert's shoulders and have set Rupert falling, it seems, into a delighted trance. I hear in Kip's voice my very own old thoughts: *A book always takes its ultimate form. Words on the page. It is the thing itself, not a record of the thing. That is, if it's a good enough book.*

*Your younger colleagues would sneer at you for saying that,* says Malcolm, shaking a finger tut-tut-tut. *Or hasn't Quissick State caught up with deconstruction?*

Deconstruction, children?

Kip shrugs and tosses back that black hair of his, so much longer but, apparently, not as long as in the intervening years he allowed it to be. *I'm out of it,* he says cheerfully. *I'm an old fart. It's a relief not to have to feel cool anymore.*

*I didn't know the world would pass us by so quickly,* says Rupert softly from his state of bliss. *I live in my moldy old pumpkin with my shelves of books that scarcely a soul wants to buy. Fine by me.*

And Henry: *Well, I hope they fill up the opera houses for another decade at least.*

*But a song has to be sung,* says Kip, *to reach its ultimate form. A book has already reached it. That's the difference. Anna, I'm your total disciple.*

*I'm too mellow for any more of this right now,* says Rupert, not opening his eyes. *All we've done this week is talk to that old dame. I loved her as much as any of you, but let's give her a rest, huh? She's exhausted me.*

*Clifford started it,* says Henry.

And Malcolm shakes his head as always. He is the one who begins so eagerly, and so serious in his questions, and then Henry and Kip, they take it away from him and off they go, answering, answering, sure and absolute and excited until my Rupert cuts them short. So it would go in the late afternoons. I would watch them across my desk, four boys in the ragged front row and empty rows behind them where otherwise would have sat all my usual lazy ones, indifferent children of that dull indifferent town. Without all those, how my classroom seemed to grow enormous, how those four chosen boys seemed like small souls in a universe of time! They did not turn to look out the two tall windows that stared at me with visions of the actual world. They saw, instead, above my forehead the dusty blackboard and its changing words. I was for them the keeper of those lines I wrote out in chalk. Ultimate form? Words must also be read, Professor Skerritt. They must not only stand there alone waiting.

Rupert leans his long thin neck back so his curly streaked-gray hair nestles in Kip's lap. Kip meets Rupert's eyes upside down. *You look so weird this way, Ru.* Rupert is spreading out his bare arms, letting them flop in the air from Kip's brown knees. Malcolm watches them, quizzically, but Henry's once again looking at the wicker ball around the ceiling light. He knows I am with them whether Rupert now allows them to talk to me or not. *Ever retrieving me, losing me, finding,* he recites.

*She comes, she goes,* says Ru. *Let's let her go now. Let's really let her go.*

*We were going to write the poem down,* Kip says. *Words on the page. Leave them here for her. We called her because we need her.*

*And then maybe we'll leave her behind at last?* Rupert wonders. But Kip says, *We'll never leave her behind. It doesn't work that way. But we'll have contacted her. She won't seem so out in the cold. She won't haunt us the same. She'll be more a part of us.*

*We'll appease her,* says Malcolm. *That's what the jumbie table is for. Keep the ancestors content. I've been reading up on it. Look, I'm getting a travel article out of this vacation so I can deduct it.*

Suddenly, Kip reaches under Rupert's arms and pulls up from behind to lift him to his feet. Rupert flops like a doll. *I'm getting some paper,* Kip says, tossing his limp friend to Henry, who breaks the fall. A scramble of boys. They are still teenagers.

But now they are opening the shuttered door to the veranda, and they seat themselves about the table by lantern light. Kip has a large shiny sheet of drawer-lining paper and a fat pen that makes broad strokes in dark purple ink. "At Graduation," he writes across the top. *One quatrain at a time,* he says. *Here, Henry, you first.*

"Now you are leaving me," writes Henry. "Go without minding, ever retrieving me, losing me, finding." He passes the pen back to Kip, who continues: "I am a mystery. Kindle my flame. All through your history, utter my name." He inspects the lines, passes the sheet to Malcolm. *Second stanza. Write it big enough, Mal,* he says. Malcolm was always the scribe of miniature notes and lists and marginalia.

"Lost as the past may seem, render it clearly." Malcolm is struggling, left-handedly, to keep his lines straight. "It, at the last, may seem candle wax merely." *What's the next line?* Rupert asks foggily, when the pen comes to him. *Think, Ru,* says Kip. No sign. Then Rupert blurts out:

*Hasten, discovering! All right, here goes, Anna, let's get this over with.* "Hasten, discovering!" he writes. "Each wick is dear. I shall be hovering, drawing you here."

*Put it under the hurricane lamp,* says Kip. *But she's not supposed to come tonight,* says Rupert. *We haven't put out the food yet.*

*If it rains, it might get wet,* Malcolm says. He's yawning.

So Kip rolls up the poem and they all get up from the table. Kip turns down the lantern and says, *It's time for bed anyway.*

*That back rub got Rupert all steamed up, I can tell,* Henry says. But what do I hear inside that voice? A certain scorn? *Let's go down to the beach, Malcolm. It's too early to go to sleep. It's Christmas Eve.*

Ah, mes chers enfants, it seems I had best find myself a churchyard and rest amongst my own kind. You need your privacy. I do not abuse my ghostly privilege, you see. I will find you again by morning light.

MALCOLM!

You are loneliest, dear one, I know. The early sun peeps in on your tight eyes. I see your teeth grind against each other in sleep and your forehead knot up. You do not know your distress. You wake troubled, not rested, not whole, but you get yourself up, hold yourself in, take the new day as it is coming to you. You have not learned to wrestle it down, Malcolm. Years ago I knew it would be a difficulty, and I worried over you. I did not help enough. You threw up excuses, Malcolm, you would not allow me to unsettle you quite. It is my regret.

If I could now enter your dreams and ease the strain in your sad face — you, the set-aside one, you have been in my thoughts all night as I sat up in the vine-hung grove of old tombs by Saint Anthony's Church. There came to welcome me a pair of vaporous slave ghosts, two centuries old — Quaco and Quashy they called themselves. It was their master's grave we sat upon. Even still they visit that stone. Quaco had been the strongest man on the island. He sold for one hundred and fifty-five pounds, and what a price that was in 1750 for a man! Quashy is still in awe of him; he had been only eighty-three pounds' worth of flesh himself.

There we were, talking like old friends in the language of the spirit. (How else could I have understood their antique African English?) Quaco, huge and black and with angry teeth, and Quashy, lean like knotted rope and with a mad smile — they are still comrades-in-arms. They pushed at each other's shoulders and slapped each other's backs and chuckled and jeered and burst into joyful laughter — then all at once, gaping at me, their latest audience, they told of ears cut off and breasts burned with fiery irons and a rebellion betrayed by a timorous slave woman. You have read these stories in the island history you have studied, Malcolm. Perhaps, visions of their tortures enter your dreams now, emblems of your own sorrow.

For all their amiability, these men told fearsome tales. How they hated the master in the earth below! His spirit, they told me, has never once emerged in all these years, his eternal soul is enslaved to the black volcanic soil while theirs roam free. This is not justice, Malcolm; it is merely the natural end of a brutality that never ached for love, for kindness, for truth. It is unsatisfied yearning that creates ghosts, child. We are yearners who still have reason to inhabit this poor place, our old world, yearners for vengeance, yearners for forgiveness. How long must my yearning sustain me here until I have completed it? Am I never to reach oblivion? Quaco and Quashy are, you may imagine, master yearners. They have sad lessons to teach me.

You, too, Malcolm? All night I have thought of you. One

day you shall become a ghost like me, no doubt. What is it you yearn for?

Your daughters, yes, I feel it too. But I have no living daughters to call me to them. I dream upon times we were all three alive and together, but insubstantial ghosts cannot satisfy each other's yearnings. You may be lucky and die before your daughters. Then you will hover about them, I assure you. But you will not bother with Martha Hooper again. You have preferred to be a father without a wife. You wish now, grinding your teeth, to strike Martha Hooper from your mind, to leave you with two motherless girls, all yours. I had no more use either, finally, for Mr. Aylmer, nor for Señor Praz in Spain, nor for Herr Ulrich, father of my little angelic one, any more than for my first passing love who left me with my Alma. But the children — what were we thinking then, Malcolm, you and I, to bring children into this world?

You do not quite dare even now ask yourself what stirs in your gentle heart. Leave it at loyalty, you tell yourself. Steadfastness. Duty. But back behind all that, still the awful lonesomeness, Malcolm.

Rupert had once come close to you, Henry closer, Kip earliest and closest of all. What did you really want from those boys, muchacho? I saw it, Malcolm, I could see it before my eyes as you sat in your bright argyle sweater, puzzling at me — they had put you in a certain place, as if you would not grow along with them.

As the ghost men told their tales of bleeding wounds, of martyrdom, I thought, strangely, of you, Malcolm. The island spread out its stars. I was somehow again in Spain. I was keeping watch with two soldiers — so it felt — dispelling the horrors of war with midnight conferences. They asked me to speak too: how was I acquainted with misery? I began to tell tales of my own. You know little of me, Malcolm. I did not impose on you boys. Now two old slaves haunting this island know more of how I lost my own first girl in Catalonia, how I never had to watch her bleeding in the bombed cookhouse but had instead to hear tell of it when there was nothing I could do, no way to get to her, to see her face again. And how I had to make my way, not home to my other child with her father in Hitler's land but to the ocean's opposite shore, to safety. Quaco and Quashy, in their spirit-minds, they have seen my life now as clearly as I have. But you, Malcolm, you twist yourself up in bedsheets, your fingers twitch at the pillow, and you dream of two young girls in a quiet back-yard in California beside a swimming pool, growing away from you. And that is misery too.

And how did you feel last night, to descend the hill with Henry and watch the starlight on the tumbling sea? To see Kip and Rupert hand in hand closing themselves behind a bedroom door? It is not a matter of man or woman, for you, Malcolm, it is more simple, I feel. It is some matter of love. I saw it then as I see it now. Your Uncle Abraham — his ghost must still be yearning in the moonlight outside some middle-aged lady's dressing room — he suffered the curse of your tribe as well.

Quaco and Quashy heard my tale, and I told them also of you, of all four of you, of why I have come here. What is my yearning to theirs, I wondered, but they assured me: ghosts do not bother to assess quantities of sadness. There is no hierarchy amongst us. As long as we find ourselves persisting, we know there is in us sadness enough still, and so we are equals. Only when the sadness shall finally be absorbed in thin air, Malcolm, are we released. Someday your yearning, too, will join our lingering company and know us ghosts as nothing more than human sorrow and its most essential component, human love. Isn't it?

He is blinking. He stirs. The small mouth opens, like a baby's, for breath, and then the eyes for light. But as he sits up he becomes again a grown man, a father, fine-boned and feather-weight but burdened as I, a mother, have been. Grüsse, Malcolm! Guten Morgen! Ki-keri-ki! Yes, by God, I do hear a rooster up the hillside, now in the silence. The waves do not crash so terribly this morning. As I talked all night with my voluble new friends, the surf subsided almost to an amorous pat upon the sand.

He looks right through me. My girls, he thinks, I dreamed of them again, and somewhere in there was, no, not Martha, but Rupert, and we were on a sunny beach in California — no, but it was last night, Henry and I, and looking at stars over the Caribbean.

He shivers, tosses thoughts from his head. He must be good to his friends again today. They have been good to him. What is it to be good? He must not question. He learned it long ago at his mother's side. In the Upholstery City he would be known for his goodness. The Phipps Pharmacy was a good place, people had known him always, they could trust him, his father would make them well. And his house was good because it was clean and without luxury and everything in it had always been part of the family. Even his Uncle Abraham, who, though not good, was pitiable, was also somehow dear. And his sister

Louisa is maybe, in some ways, as good as he could ever hope to be, because she is still there, behind the counter, and though, as time passes, the town is much changed, her old goodness still shines forth to browner-skinned customers. She belongs there, she has a birthright, her ancestors cut the very stones that shield her enterprise from the winter weather. How can I, Malcolm is thinking in a recess of his soul he is not aware of, how can I move beyond? How can I be anything but good, ever and always? Even if my daughters would never come to see me again, if Martha would turn them against me now, still I could not, could not have the thing . . . Thing, a blank word lodged as far within him as I can penetrate. He is putting on tennis shoes and lacing them up so carefully. He plans a run up the road before the others arise. There is fear in him.

You told me, children, that you were all, eventually, homosexual, and even Malcolm must have accepted the term, for I heard no familiar whiny protest. But something of it eludes him, yes? I can always tell these things. Even then. For all his eager note-taking did he not as fiercely resist me? He was the best student but the worst learner, dear ones. And now, from learning this new possible thing, some fearfulness has stopped him dead. What is there to fear, child? Do you carry with you, Malcolm, the puritan voice of Quissick and its expectations? In ghostland, let me assure you, moralistic strictures are only to be laughed at. Even I, opinionated Anna Aylmer, have learned to forget what notions I held of the natural order of man, woman, beast and flower. From my vantage point, buzzing here about your head, human judgment is paltry,

Malcolm. Come, relax. Love is an assault on the fear of death, not a courtship of it.

But you look up strangely in my direction, as though there is something unthinkable I do not know. Quickly, to escape it, you stand and slip onto the shady veranda and tiptoe past the other rooms to the corner of the house where the sun strikes the path leading up, between immense white-flowering bushes I have never before seen, to the dusty road.

And now you will regulate yourself. Your step picks up, you set your pace, one foot springing before the next in precise rhythm. No, I will not follow. He is pounding all thought from his head. Malcolm is teaching himself to meditate upon nothing at all. There I may not enter.

A GOLDEN chameleon (is it?) joins me on this concrete wall by the roadside. The sun sits up there on the volcano's left shoulder, and its light filters sharply through the greenery. Palm fronds form, for me, unfamiliar shadows, and small lizards are unaccustomed company. Is this island my final transplantation?

*I don't believe the world will get any larger,* wrote Malcolm when I asked him, once, for a prophecy. For previous assignments he had only to look back on something and tell me, methodically, all about it, so this time he must write about the future. It wasn't fair, he complained, when the others could do research. You must then research your soul, Citizen Phipps, I said.

Malcolm loved me to ask him to read aloud; he would lose himself in the page and forget his listeners. That dripping March afternoon as he read, there behind his bowed head the faint suggestion of green on the maple branches impressed itself in my thoughts. Ah, Malcolm, too, is beginning at last, I have brought him here to this point of looking hard, I told myself, and how each sentence enthralls him!

*I don't believe there will be any more room for us.* On he read, sinking deeper in his chair, but nonetheless his voice rising. He was sure: that from satellites we had now seen at once everything there was to see of earth, that we had now objectified it, so he said, pictured it from elsewhere, that soon the human eye would encompass the globe in one glance from a moon perch or speeding rocket. How small from space it would appear, a blue-green ball suspended on a black sky, not all that much larger up there than the moon had always seemed from here.

My other three boys were envisioning it with him, a sight they had never given thought to. Nor had I. Malcolm was convincing us of it: we were to ignore the technicalities that usually clutter such forecasts and instead think what the effect (earth-rise on moonscape) might do to our souls. Preachers had attempted the trick, to make us see our poor planet focused in the eye of God; poets had managed it better, and so he quoted Whitman — *"O vast Rondure, swimming in space . . ."* (Assigned by Jerry, of course.) *But to see it with the human eye,* declared Malcolm, *will be to stick us here, finally and humbly. The moon will be no enticement, no lush island colony to dream of sailing to. We will be thrown on ourselves, several billion of us, here and now.*

And then his voice rose still more, though its undertones trembled a bit and Malcolm's foot, crossed tightly at the ankle, had begun to waggle. *I believe,* this boy with knotted brow proclaimed, *that socialism will then be possible.* Henry could not stop himself from spluttering; I shushed him with an arched eyebrow, and he lowered his chin and shook his pink cheeks to let me know he would forever defend the entrepreneurial spirit that built Vigneault Lumber; those four, who always wanted to present a united front, were indeed as riven as I. Keep reading, mein Kind, I said, savoring the contentious air. *Socialism,* he read as firmly as he could, *will finally have become necessary.* Henry's fingers tapping. *Because there will be no unknown land to pillage, no new race to enslave, no heaven in sight as a reward for suffering. There will be no more money to be made, no markets to expand.* Henry wondered aloud if Malcolm had ever heard of the population explosion. I shushed him again. The sermon resumed: *When people thought the earth was flat, it might have seemed infinite, a plane with no known edges. It has kept getting smaller ever since. It may take years,* Malcolm admitted, at last raising his eyes to meet the challenge, *but I believe the earth is reaching a period of great reversal, a peripeteia, if you will, where one will begin to see differently. Change must arise from within and not be imposed by force. If the world seems smaller one year and smaller still the next and terribly small as time marches on, then I believe a shift will occur. Humanity has never regarded itself the same way for long. We must not assume that American ideas of property rights are eternal. I believe that the iron and bamboo curtains will part, no longer necessary . . .*

My Rupert had begun to protest also by gazing blankly at the wall maps. But Malcolm had never allowed himself this before, to dream his dream for us, he who never assaulted a thing, he who sealed up his fury. My request for prophecy had caused the old Uncle Abraham in him, maybe, to let loose.

But even Prophet Malcolm was still Malcolm, well ordered and cautious, and when he felt deepest then would his sentences turn most to stone. But what did I alone hear beneath the schoolboyish voice that the other three could not yet hear? The yearning, too, in Malcolm, to make again a small homeland of the world, to pursue a shared labor and accept a common debt and for one man not to strive against another but to prosper from the other's good fortune. The Spanish war raged before my eyes as he spoke, and there sat I, old rebel in retirement, ideal-seeker seeking no more but only waiting and watching, I, once the young woman dressed in men's pants, hair back in red bandanna, grime under fingernails, mud up to hips, fire of battle shining back from my eyes — was it shining again then at my boys? But how could they have seen it? For them I still had my dowdy shape, my unsteady step, my tight braid of hair tied upon my head. I was still the woman of absolute opinion, and yet somehow to them forever also the mystifier. I was of course no Republican (such as Monsieur), but then no Democrat either to hear me speak of the young president at the time. Communist, perhaps, yes, but how I hated the self-styled communists ruling half the world. And they remembered how I called my old countryman Bert Brecht a sly fox with his clever answers to the McCarthy Committee and his Swiss bank accounts. Fascist I was not, and yet I represented perhaps a fascist manner, or so certain students must have thought who once — how terrifying it was — caused that loathsome banner to descend outside my window. But what had I seen? A bloodied vision of my second child, my Angelika, on her dying day in Germany engulfed in such red flames?

Yes, my dear ones saw how for a moment I no longer knew where I was or with whom. And they are right, yes, then I did turn to them, my loyalists, they would protect me as I would have to protect them always also. They did not know why it should be so, they did not know how my blood ran with theirs, but they knew I had called them out, made them mine. And they had a sense that my mystery was a part of my teaching: I would not proclaim my own private history but only my thought, thought that could then be free.

And now here I live at last in thought alone, thought that does not speak in words. There are no words, there is no language here in this tropical air. I do not need a syntax. I do not need my bad English or my ancient German or my schoolroom Spanish. I do not need a voice under my voice. I only need to visit a thought upon them when the right moment comes.

I hear the feet of Malcolm pounding the road, and now I can see him appear at the bend, his mind as empty as he can make it, forcing him only to pound, to pound, to pound, and think of nothing. I sense for him something like bliss in it. Ah, Malcolm, I am told your iron curtain is still in place, your homeland-planet has not yet been sighted, and you find a certain relief in forgetfulness and in the effort of simply pounding on. Is that it?

He stops before me, rests his tennis shoe on my rock. The chameleon slips into the greenery. Malcolm bends to stretch his knee, his thigh, and then the other leg. He is all smoothed with sweat. And I catch his thoughts in words: They think I'm so unphysical. They think I don't let go. But I'm in better shape than any of them. My lungs breathe deeper. My heart is stronger. They don't know entirely what I've been up to either. I've made a few of my own discoveries. In a world that doesn't know the old me, where I'm not exactly Malcolm Phipps. I told Henry I wanted to take the blood test too. At first he thought I was doing it for solidarity . . .

A shout from the bungalow.

And now the sea, says Malcolm's reawakened mind, to wash me clean.

Blood test, child?

OH, MERRY *Christmas, I guess,* says Henry. I'd pretty much forgotten.

That must be a relief, Kip says, unfolding the island map across the breakfast table. *I wonder how my family's feeling, all that chaos around the tree and no Uncle Kip to organize the presents. And Oops wanted me to meet her new jock boyfriend.*

*I don't miss the Tunxet Brook Home with its aluminum tree,* says my sleepy-eyed Rupert.

*But here we have the Christmas bush,* Malcolm says, indicating the large burst of white among the green leaves beyond the veranda. *It decorates itself, at the right time of year.*

*Do you think she's here yet?* Henry says suddenly, and the others turn to him. Rupert's eyes have flared up, as if he is waking from a nightmare.

*Well, I've certainly been thinking of her a lot this morning,* Malcolm says. *I can't get her out of my thoughts. I had to go for a run to escape. Why did we go on summoning her, day after day?*

*But only during cocktail hour,* says Kip.

*I feel her here right now though,* says Henry. He looks through me where I lean against the railing, as supple again as I was when a girl. *It's like the ghost arriving at the end of* Don Giovanni. *Did I tell you I had to step in at the last moment in Spokane? The part's too low for me.*

Henry's words sit in the warm air awhile. He's afraid he talks too much about his performances, so he gets up to stand at the railing, and I return to my clearer vantage point above all four heads. It is wonderful how the body sensation comes and goes at will in ghostland, as if I may for a time pour thought into an invisible shape and then, quick, float out of it and dissolve into thought again. The living mind also might take such pleasure in mobility; I am sure it only imagines itself so bound to flesh.

*We never knew,* Henry says now to fill the long silence, *we'll never know if she could've made that turn. Or if she even wanted to make that turn. Maybe if we'd said our graduation good-byes a different way — think how she could sometimes react when we missed an assignment, when we didn't get what she was driving at. I sometimes imagine her death as a fit of rage.*

There below me, the dear heads. I feel the closeness of our souls surging into the emptiness of my first dead years, when they would not reach for me, lying alone in Quissick's earth where I had never found a true home. But not since the Kaiser's day had Anna Klumpp settled into any town in the wide world. In my last and quietest town, only the switching of railcars was my night music, the factory bells and workmen's shouts were my morning song. I had no sleeping neighbor unless a night watchman went napping. I would sit alone like a conscience, in judgment of my own self. I sat there despite my dead daughters, despite my failed politics, despite my lost old world, and held on to all that could not be said and could not be known and could not be understood and could not be forgiven. I kept those secrets, and music and books were my only intimates.

But on three nights in those last years, when Rupert was for sure at school for a dance or a play, I did venture out. I drove in my Plymouth to that inhospitable street in Plashing Falls. I rapped with my keys on that brass nameplate HUTCHINS. Eventually a light inside. And she hovered behind that frosted glass, a shadow in the pear tree etched there. The first time I approached her, some Nazi voice within her, deep under, rent her as no voice could ever rend me, and I perceived her madness. I had held all my own voices tight to me on my perch in Riverbend, so they could never surprise me as I had surprised her. She slammed the door in my face.

Such chance had led me there, such strange luck that Ruth, my old comrade-in-arms, had known since her boarding school days and all through Vassar the future Mrs. Tavistock. And that Ruth had prevailed upon her school friend to vouch for me in Quissick when I first sought refuge, separated from Aylmer, rootless, poor. For all their differences, girlhood loyalty sustained their letter writing over the years, and there was often an amusing paragraph, Ruth would report, about a German maid, Undine, and her funny way with English and her foggy brain and, later, her muddy little war orphan and then the antics of that wild boy at the farm, how the Tavistock children played games to tease him and how he seemed to enjoy the attention and let them dangle him from a rope out the hay door till he yammered the German gibberish he would not otherwise speak for them to laugh at.

One such story Ruth happened to convey to me on a soft pink evening in our later years when we were dipping peaceful paddles into her New Hampshire lake, setting a return course for the boathouse. I gasped at her idle mention of a name — Sintram. Sintram! Had I not read it in a last letter from a doomed city, a letter promising reunion in a quieter world? Of course, Sintram, a likely brother to this humorous Undine — names out of the old romances. By God, but these fabled Tavistocks were the engineers of my fate. Once, their charity had briefly alighted on me, but I had not known then how already they had also encircled my soul in their choice of nursemaids, how soon they would cinch it tight in their fostering of a motherless child. TAVISTOCK, the huge word shining in black and white paint high on the red brick warehouse, glaring at me in Riverbend across the train yards — a name, a sign, a power beyond my imagining. I lay my paddle across the bow of the canoe, while Ruth had to rudder and stroke, rudder and stroke, but kept talking in that ringing voice of hers, unseen behind me, like destiny catching me up. I could not turn to look.

Even in Spain she had known my impulsive soul and how from high to low it ruled me. To her I was always afire with hope or in an agony, to her I was somewhat crazy. My boys down there worrying themselves over my ancient despair think me somewhat crazy still. When I sang them my old marching songs, they saw in my eyes and heard in my croaking something stupefying, a resignation to fate, a capitulation. And back then with Ruth also, in our canoe — I enacted a form of abject surrender.

But she called me at Christmas when the next Tavistock letter arrived. She had endured my fears with me so often before and could always soothe them. And now she determined to help in my investigations, in my deductions, until I was certain I knew what I should do.

So Fräulein had begun to lose more of her faculties than the family cared to do without, and the bountiful Tavistocks resettled her in one of their Quissick houses, where she might send the boy to a high school large enough to go unnoticed in. Now I was to have him in sight and begin my longed-for task. I would approach him, but without revelation. I would make first for him and me a small world. But I know I was still afraid.

And then to speak with that guardian aunt; she might even be delighted at the thought of sharing her burden . . .

Ach, my ghostly yearning is aroused in these thoughts. It reaches him despite my intentions to stay mute, to shake no lampshade, rattle no shutter, break no glass. He who had been wishing me laid to rest once and finally, he feels — look at him — for a terrible moment that old Anna Aylmer is indeed in the air around him, is still penetrating his mind. He has long ago had enough of crazy old German ladies. I must not allow him to shiver like that in this heat. Basta! Forget Anna, dear one, look, quick, at that fascinating map spread before you, a magic island to be explored. You shall leave this Anna somewhere on the breeze behind you, her poem laid on this table where the map now lies, and instead you will set out with your life's companions on a holiday pilgrimage through this actual world. Where I must only listen and watch, you may still touch it all, inhale it, taste its sweetness. Those precious lower senses were the first to leave me, Rupert. And the sense of time. I forget how, while I ruminate, only a second has passed of your clock. My time is like dreams, at once instant and endless.

But my boys are still contemplating my last fit of rage, as they imagine it. For a while I had been receiving only their spoken thoughts — at cocktail hour, was it? — but now I am in range to plunge deeper. I may even perceive the stratum more accessible to ghosts than to the thinkers themselves. They are poised upon a discomfort, an unease, and I find what is under it: the reason they have been calling old Señora Aylmer to this time and place. They have spoken, so cautiously, of another death, another dead one they have told me little of. He is the other spirit in their communion this Christmas. They say they are not ready to summon him, but thoughts are free, and perhaps he is hanging in this air with me and I have only not encountered him yet.

*Yes!* Henry finds himself saying. *It is because of her death and his, together, that we're feeling this way.*

Rupert's mind snatches at a vision. Anna has retreated, and the other specter is rising whom he would rather not see.

*Because aren't we bound to feel guilt for him too?* Henry's voice persists in the others' silence; he was the least hesitant as a boy, always. *I know, me most of all,* he concedes. *I didn't mean to speak for you.*

*He was also my friend,* says Malcolm, his brow wrinkled in perplexity.

*The guilt at being luckier?* asks Kip.

*Luckier, perhaps,* Rupert says.

Malcolm nods. *Luckier, perhaps.*

*He was my friend too,* Kip says. *And Rupert's.*

*What would Anna have made of him, I wonder.* It is Henry speaking, very slowly, a picture rising in his eyes. *Would she have chosen him too?*

*Well, I doubt it,* he answers himself, but it is no longer the words I am hearing. I am moving down into the pictures rushing across their minds at this thought of Ledyard — that is his name: he is staying after school with us, he is trying to read one of these damn books of ours, *The Faerie Queene* all in green, and he has no idea what to make of it, or me. Of course, they had not known this Ledyard as a boy, so these are strange pictures of a thirty-five-year-old man amidst their teenage selves, a grown man who would rather dance than read, and this is the picture I now see too. He is dancing somewhere in a crowded place, but alone. He is slighter even than my Rupert, his eyes hugely staring. But he is all energy and they are solemn watchers; only Henry has imagined himself beside this Ledyard, trying the dance, too, but — what music is this? The swarm of people, men and women, and in such costumes I cannot always be sure, and I am perceiving the finales of Beethoven's symphonies — it is the Seventh dancing in Henry's head but in Kip's instead the *Eroica*. What sonorities! And Malcolm is hearing the Fifth, yes — but the symphonies crash against each other in different keys and tempi. Only a ghost could find it so glorious all at once. And in Rupert there is also singing, and I watch him grin wide at a bright red banner hung above their heads: THE ODE TO JOY DANCE-FREE CLASSICAL DISCO

'82 — BEETHOVEN MARATHON. In their thoughts my boys are standing in the crowd, ghosts like me, invisible, as Ledyard leaps to all the music each of them hears, and I see four overlapped Ledyards, four wiry bodies dressed tight in black, snapping every direction in a froth of dancers. He is free and my boys are not, so he dances jubilation for them.

But a sudden silence because Henry has been able to bear the sight no longer and has spoken something that has shifted them back, curiously, to Anna Aylmer — he has said: *Yes, that's why we need her now, to help us hear all these voices in us.* And here I am, back in the classroom, looking kindly down at them, muchachos, dear ones, and we are struggling once more with the "Requiem" of Friedrich Hebbel, searching for the word — the lap of love, the bosom of love, love's womb, tightly indrawn — yes, we have it. I write it on the dusty blackboard with my stub of chalk.

*Because she was always inclined to take us seriously,* says Henry. *And this is serious.* He has tears in his eyes. He is connecting now the vision of Ledyard as he was to the vision of Henry's own schoolboy self, the boy who did not yet know what his life would become or how death would enter it.

*She taught us seriousness,* says Kip. *That's what she was up to. She wanted us to get serious about something.*

*I'll tell you why it worked,* at last says Rupert. *Because in each thing we wondered about, she had us convinced she knew the unknown behind it. She would look at me and I knew she knew me in a way I didn't. It may have scared me at times, but I have to say it, I admit it, mostly it made me feel very safe.*

I AM invisible in the tight backseat between Rupert and Malcolm, the slenderer ones. It is a very small car, with right-hand drive, smaller by far than my old coupe, but we are squeezed in. I have not contemplated myself inside any vehicle whatever since my fatal crash. I remember now that first oddness of feeling airborne, weightless, suspended — my natural condition now.

My dear ones are imagining me back at their so-called jumbie table, but mashed breadfruit had little appeal, and besides it is a mistaken notion among islanders that we ghosts can actually consume food. I would rather be riding with my boys. Did I not always prefer their company? My last mortal years had so few other companions — dearest Ruth in the summers, oh, and an occasional reunion with Aylmer, long enough to remind me how fussy he was, how little he could abide my willfulness. He had served my brief purpose, and I had served his. But Ruth, she and I reached our fullest friendship late in our lives, and there was nothing more remaining to discover. I imagine she is dead now, but I doubt if she has had to linger as a ghost — not my Ruth.

This road is rough. Henry steers along the edge, careful not to swerve right in the curves. Huge fronds of palm hang over us like protecting wings. No one else is on the road; they are all at church. No, a reddish-haired black man with a donkey passes in a blur. We are entering a village and now have stopped at a gas pump outside the only store where a descendant of Quashy, if resemblance persists so strikingly over centuries, fills our tank. There is a legend on his T-shirt: I WENT TO BARBADOS ON A PUSSY HUNT. Qu'est-ce que ça veut dire? He is asking Henry jovially if the four of them are not an English rock band here for Festival. Has England such a thing as rock bands? What I recall — a dance at QHS, Monsieur Simone and I on chaperone duty — hardly promised much for the genre. The man's supposition has amused Kip, who now whispers to the backseat: *The man at the car rental thought we were CIA. I guess there's only a few reasons a foursome of forty-three-year-old men might travel together. Too bad there's no golf course on this island. Then we'd really make sense.*

*Lucky thing I could mention my girls last night or we might have been lynched*, says Malcolm right into my phantasmal ear.

*Still might*, Rupert says in the other, and Kip turns quick to give him a mild box.

But, mes enfants, I wish I could explain it to you. It is sad to me how the living worry over distinctions the flesh makes that will be of no significance when the flesh is gone.

We are off again. Henry is thinking how he used to drive the Vigneault Lumber truck up the streets of Parapet

Ridge, as twisted and treacherous as this island road. And at every crest, a lurch in his stomach, an uneasy settling. Kip — I feel it in his sorrowful eyes — is remembering his story of the mountains, but is he Kerouac or Nabokov in the passenger seat? No, he is only Clifford Skerritt of Quissick State College, Associate Professor of Comparative Literature and codirector of Continuing Education, Humanities Division. But what else is there on this earth, my dear one, but comparing literatures and continuing educations?

The questionable pavement has turned now to gravel, and we have entered another parish, for there is the stone church, Saint Peter's. Henry slows down the car with the unexpected name: Mitsubishi. Then he stops, so we may hear the Anglican alleluias.

*I would like to be singing with them*, Henry says.

We sit a little longer in the strong sunlight then roll silently on, down the hill into a village where, passing a stone bridge over a ghaut (I employ the local term), we come upon a huge hanging beef carcass draining its blood into a wooden tub. A wooden spit awaits it where a man with a crooked back stokes a fire. There will be a feast in this village of Saint Peter's, but now the skinned corpse hangs so lonesome. Rupert shudders beside me.

As we mount the next hill, the car seems filled with the thought again of their Ledyard. I am made to see him in a white room on a white bed, white in his skin, and even his eyes seem to have gone all white. He barely lifts his hand to greet Henry. The others stand back. They all watch this scene at once but from different angles of the room, which converge in me to form a madly twelve-dimensional picture, four times real. This is a deathbed they have all attended. It is not like my sudden one, passing in an eyeblink, unwitnessed; this is one they must continue to see. They have been standing, sitting, coming in and going out, watching the eyes close softly, the breaths come further apart. Behind him now is the agony. They can only watch the time stretch out between breaths, ten seconds, twenty. Will it be possible to know when the last has been taken?

And suddenly we have come to a windmill of stone upon a hillcrest. It has no blades, nothing of its wooden mechanism inside, but it has stood solid here in the hurricanes of two centuries, walls a yard thick. Henry pulls over, and everyone steps out to explore. Around behind are the grain storage rooms, converted to a modern dwelling for a time and then again abandoned. Into the mountainside has been set a swimming tank, severely cracked now and empty, ready to slide downhill. *We could buy it, fix it up*, comes from Kip. *Spend every winter here in our old age.* The familiar imagination is at work — happy family, all together in a paradise, to hold on to each other despite all. *This will be Malcolm's room, and Henry's here. Rupert and I will have the threshing floor. We could build a living room up there and a deck on top, views of this whole end of the island, the wind always blowing, never too hot.*

*Threshing floor?* says Rupert.

*Feel that wind.* Henry has stepped carefully along the outer brink of the swimming tank. It is like nowhere in Quissick, where Tunxet Mountain and the Parapet hold off the far distances. Here we look across hamlets tucked into gullies and farmsteads patchworked across these lower ridges of the volcano to the sea where northwest the rock of Redonda (Kip points it out) rides like a whaleback and beyond it the shadow of Nevis. This is what Columbus mistook for the Indies. Not Quissick's icy winter or a cool lake in New Hampshire pines but all this effulgence of palm, wind and volcano, hot green, warm blue. How many new worlds the old one has thought it discovered!

*Zu mir, du Gedüft! Ihr Dünste, zu mir!* I hear Henry singing Wagner full voice into the blast sweeping up from the shore. Rupert gives Malcolm a raised eyebrow: these overexuberant friends of ours, developers of Caribbean retirement villas, Norse thunder gods chasing away the mists — thus I translate that eyebrow.

And Malcolm worries that the loud song might offend some shepherd below, or even some sheep in such a peaceable kingdom. It is their island, not ours. We cannot purchase a ruined windmill and deposit ourselves here for our own comfort a few weeks a year; let the old stones stand empty, relic of a cruel age when black slave cut cane under master's whip. Some new world! We should not even be here. The very color of our skin reminds them of their horror. We should've stayed penitential in our own colder land.

But Kip is worried for Henry. He has not lately seen him quite so fragile and yet so determined, by effort, by art, to come back to life with his welcoming smile. Still, Kip is worried, worried, I feel it. This recent death has put his friend Henry in a kind of danger, something yet unknown he waits to discover. And Kip is worried for himself too and worried more for Rupert. Rupert is surely in danger. This thought sweeps through Kip's head with this wind. We are all in danger, three of us, maybe even four.

Child, why this unnamed thing so deeply buried? If you

have no name for it, I may only know the fear and not the cause.

Kip stretches out a hand to Henry, who makes it safely back to the stone arch of the mill. The villa dream has faded. This, now, is what we have, Kip tells himself. Don't wish for anything else at all; it may be sadder. But can I accept it? Why am I so struck with despair when Rupert says he must move out of his pumpkin, try New York maybe for a while, get away from that claustrophobic orange vegetable he lives in, away from me, away from the glances and twitches of old Undine? Why do I keep thinking of ways to hold him? Hasn't he always been elusive? And always I repeat my return to him like a retriever fetching sticks. I am a teacher and cannot learn.

We pass across the threshing floor back to — what is it? — the Mitsubishi. But Henry is happier having sung a bit. *Now, on to the volcano,* he announces. And we are rushing along a miraculous road threaded between cliffs and chasms. Rupert and Malcolm cling to their armrests, trusting Henry nonetheless. Swoop! This is a ride best suited for ghosts.

RUPERT, who leans close to my airy self on right turns, is again in the back of the Vigneault Lumber truck on the way to the Quisquabaug Ponds. But Henry drives from the wrong side, and Tunxet Mountain goes up forever into the blue sky. The ponds are down there behind us — turn back, this is a dizzying dream. The road has narrowed and turned to dirt, and only in lowest gear can Henry climb. Or am I, Rupert dreams, with some strange man who picked me up hitching out the Leominster Road? And Anna has just died and left us a poem that makes no sense to me — she shall be hovering, drawing me here. But where is here? Is the Leominster Road here? No, this is a volcano. Is she hovering now? Am I dying? Don't let me know. But it's not Anna; it's Aunt Undine who pulls me down. Why does she come into this dream? She is safe with the sick and dying in the Tunxet Brook Home. Leave her there. There. So where is here?

He opens his eyes. Malcolm is watching out the rear window as the blue waves fall soundlessly farther and farther below us.

Undine haunts me too. Yes, ghosts are haunted by the yet living; it works both ways. She still sits glaring at me from across the dining table. My proposal, offered the second time, when she did allow me to enter, to sit with her, hangs above the dusty tabletop unanswered. I know you already, she is saying. But did we speak German? It must have been. It is unimportant, now that I speak thought's common language; style has vanished while substance persists. This pleases me as I could not have imagined, I who once loved the untranslatable nuance, the poet's music. Now everything is translated in a universal instant, and the Tower of Babel has at last reached its heaven.

"Ich kenne Sie schon" is what she must have said. But I knew she did not know me, only of me, and from a mix of town rumor and her own mania. I had been a whore, or a whoremistress, I had been — still was — a communist, a spy, she said. And I was a degenerate as well, a follower of Sappho, it was all now clear because so had Missus always spoken of Ruth, that woman who pointed my way to her frosted-glass door in Plashing Falls. Ruth had a reputation in the Vassar class of 1918. Missus loved making fun. What nasty stories she told, and now you want to steal my child? He is mine thanks to Adolf Hitler, who killed my brother but gave to me his child as my own. I shall tell all of them about you. You dare to teach perversions to children in this American town? You shall be stopped if ever you touch my child. David and Michael Tavistock and my darling Esther, they will destroy you. Do you not understand how rich they are and how powerful?

I was by then back at the front door. At first it would not open. She was still screaming when the knob finally turned and I could slip out. But I would try her yet once more. Perhaps, I thought, I will catch her in a gentler mood . . .

My boys have left the car on the roadside and follow now a path up into a strange declivity between walls of gray mud, I would almost say, a path winding among pools of gray water, steam rising, and further up the slope odd yellowish vents in the muddy cliffs, which issue forth a putrid ooze, yellow, even greenish, and then turning gray like the mud. I can sense in my dear ones' noses a tang of sulfur, a sickly queasiness in their stomachs. The volcano appears to rise still above us; this ragged crater is more of a wound in its shoulder than a vacuity where its neck should be. When next it blows, it may hurl up a new peak beside the old. The contour of this island is not yet complete.

Should my boys be walking further in? It is a gray wall of hot mud only. The burbling rents could cave in, swallow them. In youth they were never so adventurous. Rupert scrambles a distance up the spongy wall, but Malcolm is calling him down. *Let him,* says Kip, *he always wanted to be sucked to death.* And why does Henry laugh so at such a thought?

Malcolm frowns: *Please, it's Christmas.* It's not really very frightening here, he thinks. He had imagined a boiling black lake with a jagged rim tossing up fiery waves and now and again a missile of molten rock like a cannonball in any unpredictable direction. This is disappointment, a smelly messy ugly landscape with no sense of apocalypse about it, only dim nagging suppressed pains and aches, barely even felt. We are not the least brave to wander here, he thinks. And he had wanted to be brave today: to step into a volcano. Once again his newspaper column will have the self-deprecating tone his readers seem to like. Phipps in the maw of Hades worried about getting gray mud on his basketball shoes. Phipps mistaken for rock star. For spy. Phipps bumbling on in the world.

He has turned around on the path, is bending to test the heat of a gray pool, makes a face, is moving on down, stepping carefully in the dry spots. Henry and Kip decide to follow and leave Rupert to his courtship of danger. By the car they will wait, but I climb up beside my careless one.

He does not know I am here. He does not know me. His aunt in her senility may have told him my tale, but from her mad mouth he would not have credited it. My third attempt with her was answered with a notarized document signed by Michael Tavistock, his lawyer, and Undine Eid herself. It declared that if Anna Aylmer, formerly Anna Ulrich, of Quissick, Massachusetts, sought to claim a blood relation with Ruprecht Eid, also of Quissick, or in any way overstepped her role as schoolteacher, then certain letters belonging to the Tavistock family and currently in the possession of the undersigned attorney would be released to the Quissick School Board. Something intimidating like that. Attesting to activities of a subversive and immoral character. A spy. A lesbian. I laughed in her face.

"Rupert says that Frau Aylmer likes to think so much," she said. "So think over this." And she began to laugh back at me, but her laugh would not stop. She wheezed and coughed and could not stop her laugh. Rupert must have had to hear that laugh every day. He hears it now again, hears it through my thought, which is piercing him, but he thinks it is the volcano making him hear these things: how, battle born, from childhood he was roared at, abandoned, held close, laughed at, roared at again, and again abandoned, how he was hung with no clothes on from a pulley in a barn, how he ran across fields to escape up a tree and sat there shivering and then was roared at once more. And in school he was stared at by angry eyes and laughed at and occasionally beaten. Until he found a friend called Malcolm. And a teacher who did not quite roar though she, now and then, had angry eyes too. But she seemed to care for him; with a smile she noticed his drooping socks. And then the other two new friends he made, Kip and Henry — but all these carings wanted so much of him, who felt he had nothing in him to give back. He had been often abandoned, often scorned. And the teacher died. And later, after years of tormenting Kip, the one of his friends who said he loved him, he tormented him still with the other one, Henry, who said they could live together awhile. And he talked it over endlessly with Malcolm, his very first friend, who wanted from him nothing at all, and he felt free because Henry, the one he now lived with, did not expect him to be always there; Henry had his own world to explore, and hotel rooms in Knoxville and Des Moines and Colorado Springs, and no complaining, but finally no — torment! There it was: Rupert missed it. His old lover Kip had gone home, defeated by the city and the universities and the doctors and the men, had settled into a drab flimsy house, had lots of work to do, and loved his students and his family, and was exasperated by his life: but he would welcome Rupert again. Why not go home? It was still home, wasn't it? He walked a road he had thumbed out a hundred times to the concrete vegetable, with its chimney stem, its jack-o'-lantern windows, its door marked only as if by knife slices in the orange flesh. A legacy had come his way from that icy creature known to him as Missus. (It was my own small estate via dead Ruth and dying Tavistock. He could not know.) But the pumpkin was soon his. There he might hide himself away but still love Kip. He might go skulking about, might slip off for a time, but still love Kip. It was a place to sell his cartons of books from, a place to hole up in, and read. And welcome a hitchhiker in the rain when no cars were passing or the biker with the flat tire or the distance runner sweating and gasping. How often I have hovered there, outside the door, traffic roaring along the Southbridge Road . . .

Rupert has had enough of daredeviltry on the crater's slope. He bounds down the crumbling clay and lands up to his ankles in muck, but a triumph is on his face. He has decided he is free again. He is leaving. He is going to New York — if anything is wrong with him. That is what he will do. He will not stay in Quissick and torment Kip. He will disappear.

But what if he is all right? A shadow like a stray kiss from a cloud that has wandered from the mountain's cloudy peak passes over Rupert's face. If he is all right, will he stay? And if Kip is all right, as he surely is?

Why can't we know yet? he thinks, plodding down the path after his friends. He hates to wait for anything. He wants to know everything now all at once.

There they sat (I am seeing into Rupert's memory) in a bare room of white concrete blocks and red plastic chairs.

One at a time, by numbers, they were called, and each of
my boys, alone, was taken to a different cubicle where a
different kindly young woman spoke to him of the significance of knowing. To know is not always better than not
to know. You must be prepared (she is telling Rupert yet
again in his thoughts) for the knowledge you may receive.
Slowly, cautiously, he is nodding. They had all promised
they would do this, to honor Ledyard they would all four
do this together, for Ledyard had some years ago received
his own knowledge of mortality (What angel of death is
this you're dreaming of, child?) and knowing what he
knew, what we all shall know, eventually, of our worldly
estate, had led his life in grace and beauty (Rupert is thinking), and like him, like Henry's friend, I must also embrace
what is given to me, must find a way to be graceful, to hurt
no one. "If we all four together . . ." In this memory of a
cold white cubicle, Kip's voice lingers in Rupert's roaring
mind. "Yes, Malcolm too, for solidarity, though he claims
it's possible and he wants to be sure. We'll drive in to
Boston, to Beacon Street, and Henry will be back in town
for that *Enfance du Christ* thing, and we'll all go at once.
It'll be our blood brotherhood, Ru. Old friendships, still
here, reassuring each other." And then the notion of a
flight across the sea, of Professor Howard's empty villa
theirs for the period of waiting. Why not take this vacation
in our last innocence? The young woman is still looking
into Rupert's eyes. It is confidential, she is saying. He will
be known only by his number. In two weeks he will return
and see her again. This gentle young woman in the Public
Health Department, it is her job. Rupert sees her face now
wherever he turns his head. He has seen it when he sleeps,

when he watches the thunderous waves, and now when he stares at the gray walls of clay hemming him in. (My child, I did not know. There is an epidemic. I would protect you . . .)

He stops to smell a yellow gurgle from a crack in the cliffside as he passes. If this were the cure to all, he is thinking: to breathe in the stench, put it in little bottles and heal the world. This blighted chasm could be a miraculous place.

He feels suddenly better. (My ghostly arms cannot keep from reaching round him like a blanket. Yes, it is true, he is more my child than the others. It is not his character that has drawn me to him — perhaps, even, I am not as fond of his character — but it is his familiar flesh.)

May he not feel alone. May he feel he has something. I cannot do more for you now, child. Oh, how much more I could once have done for you!

WE ARE now behind God's back, as it is called, this hamlet down the mountain's far side where the road but barely reaches and no one goes by. We have turned wrong, meant to go up the Atlantic shore but ended in a farmyard. Malcolm is telling them of the island's first prime minister, born behind God's back and made a knight of the British queen. Not really a communist, no, but a man of his people, a strongman as they dub his sort, noble and somewhat fearsome at once. But still only a deputy, not free to work his will except at the whim of a white land. *And the current prime minister,* Malcolm goes on, *is no revolutionary at all. He wants to develop a new dependent trade in pale northern bodies looking to get browner.*

Henry is turning the car, but no one has emerged from these shut-up little houses of stone in the improbable knight's dusty birthplace. Or do they watch us through the slats of their windows? Who could have driven here on Christmas Day? they wonder. But, of course, a mistake, those ghost white faces are departing from behind God's back, having brought nothing we need, having left nothing but stares and pity. Do not come back.

There is still one road to be traveled. We pass a low spot, a green-gray swamp filled with egrets, beautiful awkward birds, standing there, waiting in sunlight and shade. And then we ascend again, the outer hip of the island. I am thinking of Mörike's poem now — ancient waters rise about your hips, child, and before your godliness bend down kings who are your retinue. I send the song ahead to enter Henry's skull in German. Yes, he knows it, of course — my land that shines from afar . . . *Henry, not again*, groans Rupert. The song breaks off. *But I was inspired. I heard it in my head.*

*"The isle is full of noises, sounds and sweet airs that give delight and hurt not,"* says Kip dryly.

They are always the same, thinks Rupert: Malcolm talks history, Henry sings, Kip quotes Shakespeare. And he wonders what it is Rupert does. At times — now, it seems — he has no idea. I can see the thought of his last mocking paper for me has passed through his mind. That is what Rupert does, he thinks. He unsettles.

I must lean my insubstantial body close in to Rupert's side as he thinks these thoughts. There are memories I do not wish to partake in, but a ghost is not afraid. It is why I have come here, child, to be reminded of this. He knows how he could stun me. He wanted to see how far he could go in being my rebel. Rupert?

His face is somehow blank now. My hesitation has shut him up, so I must press his thinking upon him, for both our sakes.

It was a May day, bright again as summer, and we would not be together in that way again when the month was out. I was already doing what I could to counter the mad-

woman. I had gone to Mr. Phipps, ostensibly for a medicinal syrup, but I asked offhand as he gave me the bottle
where I could best seek some business advice, and he said
with his Yankee twinkle that he was just a small town
pharmacist himself, but of course Kip Skerritt's father was
some sort of tax lawyer and the Skerritts would do anything for me. I would have headed down to Mr. Skerritt's
office on Market Street next, but was he not also Cato's father? He had surely heard of me from both sons, but which
was he himself more like? No, I decided on the Vigneaults,
who had always courted me so. "We're eager to show off
our view. We're house-proud, I admit. Won't you come
visit us up on the Ridge, Señora?" And if the Tavistocks
were powerful then no one in my camp was more so than
the man who owned the lumberyard. Vigneault would
enjoy a scrap with the old lords of town. A Québecois,
after all.

But I hadn't resolved quite yet to go. After graduation, then, when my place in the boys' lives would have
changed. I looked across the mess of books and papers on
my desk, and there was Rupert with the final paper he
would write for his old teacher. He did not seem to be
wearing socks at all, I saw when he stretched out his legs
and stretched also his delicate wrists beyond his cuffs in
preparation for reading. Plaid shirt buttoned wrong. Collar
flipped up on one side. His smudged fingers grabbing at the
pages and ripping them from his notebooks, leaving ragged
crenellations like a ruined medieval wall all along one
side. He shook the pack, pressed it out, and as he read held
up one page at a time and slapped it down, one after another, on the empty desk chair next to his own.

*The baby is the worst creature on earth,* he began. *It wants everything. It does disgusting things, but we convince ourselves that those spit bubbles coming out of its lips are cute. And yet we spend years trying to reform the baby. We tell it what it may not have. We shut up its loud drooling mouth. We make it eat when it doesn't want to and wait awhile when it does. We stop it from touching itself in the wrong places. We make it control its delightful excretions. And we have a reward we offer called love. This is an elaborate trick. On all of us. If we really loved the baby as a baby, we'd leave it be. If the baby was really loved, it wouldn't have to do anything special to feel it. But most babies get tricked and go on to trick the next set of babies.*

He looked up to catch my eye, to see if I was enjoying his wit. I was trying to, a nervous smile on my lips. Henry was sniggering. He couldn't believe Rupert was fooling again. Malcolm looked merely bored, Kip worried.

*But!* Rupert raised his voice to a new key, slapping the previous page on the neighboring desk and widening his eyes so that not one of us was sure if this usually quiet boy was being cheerful or outraged. *But the horrible selfish devouring baby is never really lost. Some former babies keep their traditions through life. Only then does it become apparent how monstrous the baby has always been. The adult baby has the power to destroy worlds. The adult baby, the one who was never seduced by that trick of love's rewards, this adult baby —*

No, child, I cannot hear it again. Even I, a ghost. It was your reproach, although you could not know it. I had come so late. I had so little to give. Henry's giggles allowed me

to snap at him instead of you, Rupert. "But really, mon en-
fant," I added, "you are too silly, all of you are too silly
today. It is the May weather. I shall blame the blue sky."
And I stood and walked, as heartily as I could, past them to
the back of the classroom and hurled up the window with
its clanking counterweights, and in came the rush of
spring. I needed that air. I was somehow choking maybe.
Out there in the schoolyard were three girls, sitting on the
granite slab with the names of Quissick High's war dead,
whispering together, the girls of Jerry Davenport, lingering
in the sun.

It was truly the end of semester. There would be no
more seriousness in these seniors. What we had done together must have already been done by then. I had awakened that day not knowing yet that it was over.

"Muchachos," I said, "it is now for me to write something for you. I give myself the assignment. Anna Aylmer,
you must write a poem entitled 'At Graduation' and have
it for your four pupils by next week at this time, which
shall be our last class together. Have it in four copies.
Neatly typed. But perhaps a manuscript in pencil scrawl
shall be torn out of a notebook and given to Herr Eid because he never goes to the typing room himself and should
not expect me to."

Rupert hung his head, all in good humor. But Kip had a
sadness on his face in his dark eyes and drooping lips and
heavy black brows. I remember.

AND NOW we have come up a broad back of land, and between us and the ocean extends a long meadow of dry grass rolling down acres before it breaks at the sea cliff. And there stands an unpainted wooden plantation house, abandoned, with a wide front porch looking not to sea but back across the road and up the hills to the steep wall of the volcano, loftier it seems and more irregular from this aspect than from the other side of the island where Professor Howard makes his home.

*We have to get out,* Kip says, and even before Henry has stopped the car, the passenger door is open and Kip is striding toward the collapsing old house, breathing deep in the fresh wind, and gazing down the tumbling meadow where goats clip at grass and a small boy sits under a twisted tree watching over them. *It's the most beautiful place I've ever been in,* Kip is shouting. *Look, every direction, mountain, grass, sea, house, goats, boy, sky . . .*

The others are coming now to meet him. Malcolm has the map in hand, folds it in the flapping wind so only the northeast quadrant shows. *This must be what's called*

*Lookout Yard*, he says. *This dot is that old house. There's nothing else around here.* And Malcolm thinks of the Italian sailor passing through that channel and giving a new name to this one of so many islands, the name of a monastery on a Spanish mountain. And thinks of Irish exiles supplanting the indigenous people, who had called the place Alliouagana. Thinks of traders bringing Africans in chains. Thinks of sea battles with the French, thinks of lime groves and hurricanes. Malcolm would like to feel all of history like this, to stand in the very spot and know it.

And now the same history persists in the mind of an old German woman, dead and soon to evaporate from her last essence on earth. Her yearning is changing now, reabsorbing itself in the truth of things. Nothing true is lost. She has said it herself.

Kip plops down on the grass. *It's not like at Howard's here*, he tells Henry, who comes and sits beside him. *The wind must keep it swept clear of all but that scraggly tree. I like it even better than that windmill for our future house. What, no song?*

*I'm sung out*, says Henry.

*Some things command silence*, Kip says.

This pleases Henry, I see. He is stretching himself out now, closing his eyes, is feeling himself in the long grass with the sun upon him and the strongest of his friends next to him, the one he now counts on most. Does Kip even know this? He does not stop, in his worries, in his eagerness, to notice how he is depended on.

Malcolm and Rupert are inspecting the plantation house. Kip only watches the grass in the wind, how it sweeps up from where the land drops off to the dancing ocean. It is so beautiful to him because it looks like the very edge of the whole world. Kip is no longer a poet now, except in the privacy of thought where poetry comes wordlessly to rest. I see how his spirit is breathing in, breathing the wordless poem of creation, and this when such sadness is also coming to him, and coming to Henry, who raises himself on an elbow, turns and shading his eyes asks, *Were we so silent after Anna Aylmer died?*

Kip remembers: *We didn't see each other much that summer, did we, we didn't all go to Quisquabaug together anymore. I went with Ru and we only fought. Malcolm was busy. You were busy. Even I was busy taking classes. Ru was his own kind of busy. We were sure it was suicide no matter what the* Quotidian *said. We'd seen her despair even if we weren't sure what was behind it. We must have been afraid to talk. I know the death itself scared us, but it was the thought of her alone, without refuge, the thought of us leaving her, the end of something that we wanted to end as much as we had loved it — how could we speak of it to each other?*

*Maybe it was just her bad driving, Kip.*

Kip is silent. He is lying in the place he feels is the most beautiful on earth. It is, perhaps. Right now I feel it is too. He has his small family with him. And it is Christmas but one of his own making, no Connel and Coral, no Io and Cato and whatever has become of Oops in these twenty-five years. He has tried to do what I would most have had some soul in this old world do for my rebellious orphan, even if it is only half reciprocated. In his sad eyes all this beauty . . . *It's strange,* he says at last to Henry, *how that little boy with the goats is ignoring us. He doesn't come*

*up to talk. I waved but he didn't respond. We might as
well not be here.*

And in a few minutes, it is true, they will not be here,
they will not ever be here again, though Kip, in the midst
of this sad thought, cannot help but scheme how they
could buy that rotting old house, paint it in soft Caribbean
colors, flowerpots all over the porch and friends together
every winter to talk and read and lie in the sun.

WE DRIVE the last leg home. There, by daylight, is the old cemetery where I passed the night. Quaco and Quashy are not there. Each has gone to his jumbie table where his progeny still honor him. And I am going to mine. What messages have Quaco and Quashy left for the living? That they rest easier now. That love has kept their embers warm.

What was my body? I try to remember it as it was in life, precisely my person at the moment. But when it died and decomposed then all its past revived in thought, and I felt my person reborn in any number of remembered bodies, as in old photos, year by year. I no longer credit only one body. In memory, my body is as mutable as thought: my body in the Spanish camp as true as my aching body at my desk in the classroom or leaning out my apartment window to greet my boys, my young dancing body in Berlin after the First War, the arms of my body dipping a paddle in a New Hampshire lake, my lonesome body come first to Quissick and working on translations at the library for my war work when I was not at school. Even my baby body,

which no one living can remember but which exists in im-
perial Germany as true as my broken body in the jack-
knifed front seat of my dangling Plymouth. Nothing true
is lost.

I did not know what I was doing. I had left them only
with their poem. They had read it, beginning to understand but not seeing at all the secret I had disclosed there.
I had woven it carefully into the lines so that, fearful and
reluctant as I still seemed to be, I could not now turn from
my purpose. It was already written.

I would have called Henry's mother, but I did not want a
fuss made. I would simply drop by, after supper, in the
American fashion. If the well-known Vigneault Cadillac
was in evidence, I would stop. Henry was working evenings now and would not be there; the younger ones, Guy
and Blanche, I had not met in school, for surely they took
French. And I would ask Père Vigneault to speak privately
with me on a business matter, and Maman would bring
me a cordial and some biscuits.

These were my very last thoughts, my last nervous
imaginings, for venturesome as I usually was, I was now
unsure. Might it not be more kindly to remain to my boys
simply Anna Aylmer, their teacher?

Coming up the Ridge, turning, I caught the setting sun
shot out from the notch in Tunxet Mountain. It blinded
me through my dusty windshield, and I did not see how
short the street was and how it curved suddenly right. And
I pushed the pedal hard, to climb, I thought, the next bend,
but there was no such road. I was over the lip of the Parapet and dropping into shadowy treetops. And still they believe it was on purpose, because of my despair.

THE CHAMELEON is again on the wall. He scuttles off as they pass, single file, into the bungalow. I glide instead above the roof and down over the veranda with its jumbie table.

The visitation is supposed to have occurred, but the table still bears its mashed breadfruit in a green bowl and its poem on drawer-lining paper. How serious is all of this to them? They do not believe there are ghosts. They are psychological. For them, my spirit is only in each of them, a thousand tangles in a corner of the brain calling up the days of youth in a creaky dusty cavernous classroom, calling up a way of talking to them about their own words, to say what they mean, feel what they know, hear what they had not yet heard. My ghost, dear ones, is but a somewhat different configuration in each of your brains, electrical in impulse but not sufficiently charged, you think, to draw kindred electricity from the graveyard up in snowy Quissick.

The bowl with its mound of colorless mush sits just in the shade of the roofline beside the white sheet of dark words where my secret lies hidden. I have, in ghost-time, hours to contemplate what I must do before the slatted door opens below me and I see their faces fall: the breadfruit has not been touched nor the poem read. Now they must resume, intermittently, their fond and exasperated thoughts of an old dead woman until with time she fades. This must be my last best moment with them. They will not think of me again so much all at once.

With the force of my thought I must now pierce each mind, now or not at all, a moment of reversal, as if an automobile is braking, but, oh God, too late! You are first falling ahead then sinking back, the stomach all hollow, that is how it feels.

This sunlight falls by some chance, perhaps, straight along the margin of the poem and completes for you my story, children. The door swings open, and my four dearest ones come forth.

### At Graduation

Now you are leaving me.
Go without minding,
Ever retrieving me,
Losing me, finding.
I am a mystery:
Kindle my flame,
All through your history
Utter my name.

Lost as the past may seem,
Render it clearly.
It, at the last, may seem
Candle wax merely.
Hasten, discovering!
Each wick is dear.
I shall be hovering,
Drawing you here.

*She hasn't come.*
*We'll have to eat it ourselves.*
*Look, Rupert, in the sunlight. There's a name!*
*A name?*
*No, read the first letters downwards.*
*N. G. E.*
*Start with the title.*
*Angel? Oh no!*

The seventeen letters of his mother's full name, American-style so he will understand them, shine out at the edge of the roof's shadow.

*We have been visited,* says Malcolm, knotting his brow tight, his gentle face in some kind of deepening pain. Rupert stands staring, Kip's arm on his shoulders. Henry turns from them and looks out to the waves that come pounding in, it is true, like the assault of cannon on Barcelona, one after another, or like what must have rained upon Cologne nearly forty-three years ago, killing, I thought then, the last of my blood.

I know now, when I lay then alone in my narrow bed and heard the trains coupling and big trucks loading, that what I perceived as only the thought of my Angelika, constantly in my midnight mind, was in fact she. She had wafted there to Quissick and would watch me as I now watch my boys. And so too my Alma must have watched me in America at the first, in huge Chicago with convenient Aylmer, at Ruth's quiet lake — but Alma did not need to linger. A simple good-bye, for she had come to know me truly in life; we had completed our task together. Angelika I never knew. Ulrich kept her for his own from the start. I cared hardly enough for her. She was a child in school uniform when I saw her last, a girl falling in love when last I heard from her. In such a body, rather than as the young mother I had known nothing of, she would have appeared in Quissick had I been able to see her. But, as a ghost, she had little time for me. She had to attend instead to her son, sitting on a rooftop not far away, telling his new young friends about her, each picturing her differently but always with an aspect of Rupert in her, his gray eyes, his curls, his delicate nose, wrists.

And now? But no ghost yearns for merely another ghost. We only pass, indifferent, by each other with sometimes a tale or two of a time gone or, like those rebel slaves, we sit on the graves of the unghostly unyearning dead and suffer out our hatred till that too dies.

I must take my pain only from these living ones. They cannot know I had meant to leave them in a safer world.

*She is still here with us,* Rupert says slowly. He is feeling me in the line of sunlight down those initial letters. He has not touched the page to move it, but the world is turning to the east and the fixed sun will touch the next letters soon and then begin to illuminate words and finally a whole poem and they will read it again and again and ponder the voices beyond my last lesson with them.

The halls of Quissick High were so quiet because all but my boys had gone to the fields to play or gone home to sit on sunny front porches and dream back on their years in school now ending. But for Malcolm Phipps, Clifford Skerritt, Henry Vigneault and Rupert Eid, only these words from me, three typed copies and a messy manuscript, like my chalky blackboard erased and written over and underlined in harder sharper strokes until the voice is captured exactly right. There it is. That is what it means.

I did not know I would so soon be dead. But it is wise to keep death in mind. My poem helped me prepare myself.

Now you are leaving me. No, not that they would take flight from Quissick and never return. Not that I would not meet them again for coffee at Boyle's or read Malcolm's bright articles or the promising stories yet to be written by Kip, or hear Henry, after his recent success as the Arcadian shepherd, go on to sing perhaps Kurwenal and Posa someday. Or hold my grandson Rupert in my arms as I had yearned to from the moment I picked him out, so odd, in the study hall lost in some Dickensian orphanage. But they, as they were, were leaving me. Those boyish forms of them were leaving, that moment of them that I would always especially love.

Go without minding. Do not heed me, you must not if you are to be grown. You must listen now instead to the voices in you that I have striven to make you hear, and you must not dwell in this past with me but only cherish it.

Ever retrieving me, yes, as now. Losing me, as you have, finding again. But for a moment only? I am a mystery. And I am still, my dear ones. Harder to know now, this moment, than I ever seemed then. This one child for whom I collected a family in my own name can only be thinking that I have hurt him far worse than he imagined. I knew who he was, I alone, and did not tell him but left him to struggle with that awful aunt, left him to her. My punishment is coming. I must listen to it, close, inside his mind as he sleeps tonight, and then at last my essence may finally escape, up the volcano's slope to the clouds that always hover there, saturated with the god's tears.

Kindle my flame. You have done so. Like my compatriots at their jumbie tables, I have received the honor of your memories. All through your history — yes, Malcolm, history. It is yours now too, as you have said — utter my name. But not my name exactly, children. I did not mean the name Anna Aylmer, born Klumpp. Even in our classroom, despite the spring breeze, you began to feel what I meant: the name of one who teaches.

Lost as the past may seem, but not when you tell stories of it. Render it clearly, for all stories are about time and in stories all time continues to exist and there is no present. Stories are our great refuge, isn't it?

It, at the last, may seem candle wax merely. How this sentence troubled them, as they read it over, the notion that the past is but a sheath for some inner thing that runs through it, a delicate thread about to burn. *But, Frau Aylmer, a candle burns down, not up,* said Kip in protest. *The flame is really at the beginning of it, not the end.* Hasten, discovering! Yes, child, for every metaphor there must be a precise meaning. That is what literature is for. I have told you. *But how can the past be a thing that hasn't happened yet?* he asked. Ah, how each wick, each life-thread of my boys, is dear. When we fought it out, when I wrestled with them, then it was good, then I had no fear for them.

I shall be hovering. Yes, as a flame hovers over a candle, as a death goes before. And you, children, still lie encased in that which melts away. I am drawing you here from above, my children, drawing you in to your last centimeter of ash. I am not death, however, my dear ones, my dearest ones, but I was life. And now I have said so to your deepest souls that do not yet hear me because there are strange tears in your eyes clouding your thoughts, which are also of Ledyard, I think (yes, at last, Henry, run to your bed and lie down weeping on it — now!), and of two skinny daughters out of place in a small Back Bay apartment, and of a boarded-up concrete pumpkin on a roadside with its faint flapping sign — Old Books — and its one inhabitant perhaps escaped again, and of an unknown despairing grandmother plunging her 1939 Plymouth over a granite cliff without enough time to think again of what she had once begun.

But you will all read my poem at a later time and hear yet deeper voices inside you. *We understand*, you will say. But too late.